CONVICTION

THE CHARITY DEACON INVESTIGATIONS
BOOK 8

PERRY WILSON

Ebook ISBN: 978-1-990509-26-1
Paperback ISBN: 978-1-990509-27-8
Audio book ISBN:978-1-990509-28-5

FREE EBOOK

Claim your copy of Buying Into Death when you use the QR code to sign up for my newsletter and follow Charity as she solves her fastest case yet!

Or... Head over to www.pawilson.ca/mysteries and sign up.

I balanced baby Theo on my hip while Lu finished filling a plate with pastries. Motherhood hadn't changed her at all, still elegant and immaculate as ever. The kitchen was a showplace of gleaming stainless steel and stone. How did she manage to keep that up with a baby?

Matthieu poured wine, a very small glass for each of us since none of us were day drinkers, and we were gathered to wet the baby's head. Theo burped. I looked down to see a mess on my tee shirt.

"I'll get you something to change into," Lu said. "Matthieu, take Theo. Charity won't want to eat with sick on her boob."

In minutes I was wearing a black tee from Lu's closet, my own sealed in a plastic bag to contain the toxicity.

"I'll be glad when he's over that stage," Lu said. "I'm usually in sweats and an old cotton top. I get dressed up for visitors, but it's always a risk."

So, motherhood had changed her, at least when no one

was looking. "You don't need to wear fancy clothes for me," I said.

"Believe me, I look forward to it. I like knowing my favorites still fit. I'm afraid that wearing baggy old clothes will encourage me to get fat."

"You'll get plenty of exercise when Theo is mobile," I said. They would be buffering every surface in the house soon.

Back in the kitchen, Theo was fast asleep in his car seat, which doubled as a cradle, and Matthieu was munching a chocolate tart.

"Do you miss France?" He'd move to Canada for Lu, and they'd spent the last year in *Pina Sur Midi*, where he used to be a gendarme before quitting in disgust at the corruption he saw all around him.

"We can visit any time," he said. "One of the benefits of being self-employed."

"Speaking of which," I said, reluctant to ask my question when he seemed so relaxed. "When are you coming back to work?"

He could stay home and live off Lu's money, but Matthieu liked investigating, even the boring work for insurance companies.

He glanced at Lu as if for support. "I will, but not yet," he said. "I want to be here for Theo and Lu."

"We don't have a big caseload right now. I can manage it as long as I don't take on much new business." What else could I say? My own parents had dumped me with relatives to go do good around the world. They died overseas and it was months before we knew. Theo deserved a closer bond.

My phone vibrated. I checked the caller ID: Rance MacDonald. Hotshot lawyer and father to my friend Val's boyfriend. I didn't see Val much anymore now that she was in a relationship and running her own business. Neither of us high-powered entrepreneurs had much time to socialize.

"I'll take it in the living room," I said. I grabbed a pastry and a napkin and headed out of the kitchen.

I accepted the call.

"Hold for Mr. MacDonald," a female voice said right after my hello.

"Charity," Rance said moments later. "How's business?"

"Good." Rance was a partner in one of the biggest law firms in Vancouver. He didn't reach out to lowly private investigators for a chat.

"Can we meet?" he asked. "I want to run a case by you. If you have capacity to take something on, that is."

"I do," I said, despite Matthieu's absence. I couldn't really turn away business. "But don't you have an in-house team?"

"They're on another case. I'll tell you everything when you get here. Is eleven at my office good?"

"I'll see you there," I said, and we ended the call. The timing would give me a chance to drop by my place to change into something more appropriate for a downtown law office than capri jeans and a borrowed tee.

I tucked my phone back in my pocket. If this was a big job, I could manage it, just about. The cases still on my plate were mostly reports and research; Matthieu could do that from home and still be there for his wife and kid.

This was what I wanted after the last case. To work on normal PI jobs. Sure, I'd hoped it would be with Matthieu, but that would come. No vicious gangs. No dangerous situations. No cops involved.

I popped the pastry in my mouth and used the napkin to catch any crumbs. Then I noticed the mess on the floor. Unlike the kitchen, in here baby blankets lay where they'd been tossed on the sofa, a pile of clean diapers sat ready for use on the coffee table, and a suspicious stain lurked on the carpet. Gone was Lu's showplace. Little Theo had already made his presence known, and he wasn't even crawling yet. For some reason, the mess made me happy.

"Rance may have a job for us," I announced as I reentered the kitchen.

"A law firm is a good bread-and-butter client," Matthieu said. "Is that the right expression?"

"Yes," Lu answered him.

A bread-and-butter job could easily take all our capacity. It felt a little too much like working for someone else to make me happy.

"If that's what he's offering, we'll need to talk," I said. "We don't have the capacity to take on another steady client. Maybe it's time to expand?"

Matthieu did that French shrug thing that could mean yes, no, maybe, or 'the world is an interesting place full of surprises'.

"I'm not dropping the insurance clients, or working for someone," I said. "We are independent, right?"

"Don't jump to conclusions," Lu said. "Life isn't always what you expect. Look at us, I didn't think I could love anyone again, and yet, here I am remarried to a great guy, and I'm a mother. Just let things happen for a while, Charity. And you? Living with this David guy. A cop of all things. When do we get to meet this man who convinced you to look past his job and get over the last love of your life?"

"Soon." I drank my wine and grabbed a croissant. Letting life carry me along wasn't my thing. But she was right. I didn't know what Rance wanted, so I should stop making contingency plans for something that might not happen. And I definitely shouldn't start worrying if Lu would like David. Or what I'd do if she hated him.

R ance's office was pretty much what I expected. The desk was a slab of wood on metal legs. That makes it sound far too basic. The wood was some reclaimed barn boards and the metal re-purposed railing from some fancy Victorian balcony. The client chairs were comfortable and functional designs, his chair ergonomic. No wall of bookshelves with law books lined up — probably because everything was online and had been for decades.

A painting of a Vancouver street in the rain hung above a credenza. A coffee table with a leather couch filled the space behind me. The square footage was twice as big as the whole downstairs on my floating home. Nothing like large offices to scream success in the downtown Vancouver real estate market.

"Charity, thanks for making the time to meet with me," Rance said as he strode into the room. In his fifties, he looked younger. I guess being successful helps keep the stress off your face. That, and he'd been a marathon runner for years. Confident, good looking, and per Val's comments, kind. If I was up for murder charges, I'd want him on my side like he'd been for her.

"You mentioned the case was urgent," I said, rising to shake hands.

"Yes, well, maybe not urgent to anyone but me. The trial will be months away, but I'm worried my client might do something foolish if we don't act fast."

A fast case suited me. Anything with a distant deadline usually meant more time in front of a computer than I liked.

"So, what's the case?"

"Right to the point," Rance said. "Okay. I can't give you much right now. Confidentiality issues. I'll need you to sign an NDA before I tell you who and what, but I think my client is being framed for the crime. If you can prove it, then we won't go to court, and I won't be worried about her making it worse."

I got that he wanted to be careful, but I could probably figure out the details by doing a search of public records — or even news reports. "I haven't signed one before," I said. "I'll need a lawyer to look it over first."

"Do you have one?" He didn't take offense at my suggestion that he couldn't be trusted. Perhaps it was normal in his world.

"I can get one pretty fast."

"Okay, as long as we aren't delayed too much."

That seemed odd. I guess I expected him to recommend someone in his office to go over it.

"I'll read it over first, maybe I won't need legal advice."

He nodded and turned to retrieve a two-page document from the credenza which was made of reclaimed wood full of holes where big nails had been pulled out. "This is the form. It's to make sure you keep the details between us."

I didn't say that was the usual expectation with a client.

None of mine up to now had been lawyers. The charges, client name, and lawyer were public record, so there was only so much I might reveal that couldn't be found easily.

"I'll give you a few minutes," he said, then strode out of the room.

I always envied that particularly male walk. Not arrogant, just confident. Must be in the hips somehow. All the men in my life seemed to know when to do it and when to turn it off. When I walked confidently, I always felt like I should be wearing a dominatrix outfit. Maybe it was just me.

The form was straightforward. I couldn't discuss the details of my investigation with people outside the law office, and specifically with David or Leigh. I usually got my inside information on cops from either of them, so that might slow me down a bit. I didn't see anything much different from my own client agreement form.

I didn't want to just go ahead and sign after suggesting I needed legal advice, so I reached out to David. Not that he was a legal expert, but as a cop, he might know something about investigating a frame-up. I'd already decided to take the case, but I didn't want Rance to know it was that easy.

"Hey, Charity," David said.

"Got a minute?"

"Two, in fact," he said.

I told him what Rance wanted and asked if he saw any pitfalls before I signed.

"Who are you and where is Charity?" He laughed.

"I know, but I'm trying to be better at asking for help. I won't be able to get police files from you or Leigh, and I'm pretty sure I'll need some kind of access to the investigation."

"Rance should have that," David said. "Look, he's a good

guy. He gets his clients off charges, but I think that just forces us to be better at our job. Go with your gut."

I told him I loved him and ended the call. This not-going-solo all the time was confusing. He probably guessed I was taking the case anyway, so no point in pushing my buttons.

The office door opened, and Val stuck her head in. "Charity, I heard you were in the building." She looked over her shoulder and then slipped in and closed the door behind her. "Are you going to work with Rance?"

Val and I had a weird, sister-like relationship. Since I found her actual sister when they were both working the streets, she'd relied on me, and pushed me away all the time. As she got older, the pushing away became less harsh and more like independence. She runs her own business now, organizing people and offices. She'd been digitizing the old files for the law office for a few months.

A question bobbed up from the suspicious part of my brain. "Why isn't he using the in-house investigators?"

I'd asked him, but Val's information would help me understand why Rance was really looking for external help — did he think the frame came from his office? One of the other clients?

"They're tied up with a big class action right now," she said. "I don't get details, just gossip."

"Did Rance send you in here to convince me to take the job?" Once awakened, the suspicious Charity didn't go back to sleep easily.

She just laughed and pulled the door open. "Does it matter?"

I couldn't help but laugh with her. "Maybe."

She gave me a double thumbs up and left.

Rance came back with two coffees only moments later. "So? You probably have questions."

"I signed the NDA, but I need more information before I take the case for sure."

He put one of the coffees in front of me and sat back. "It's Joan Tiller. You must have heard of her." He paused to give me time to admit I had no clue who she was. "Big deal in the small-time criminal gangs. I know you've dealt with some big bad players, but there's a group of smaller, more community organized gangs. Not good guys, but definitely not into the hard-core crimes."

So not selling kids or other kinds of people trafficking.

"What's the charge?" I figured it was serious if she'd come to Rance.

"Murder. One of her thugs who might have been working with the police, or her competition, it's not clear."

"And why do you think she's being framed?"

He leaned forward and placed his elbows on the desktop. "There are irregularities in the files. You need to meet her. Can you stay for a while?"

I had nothing better to do. "If she's ready now, yes."

3

Rance made a call, and a second or two later a woman pushed open the door, stood for a moment, and then chose the chair beside me. It all felt like an act. Like she considered forcing us to move to the coffee table and couch arrangement, then deigned to join us at Rance's desk anyway.

She didn't need to act like she owned the world; her stature did that for her. I'm five eight and she was a head taller than me. Rangy and rawboned, her appearance made her a presence. She'd had some work done, but it didn't disguise the fact she was aging. A bit of tightness around her eyes gave me the idea she must be in her sixties.

She looked me in the eye and then from toe to hair. If I had to guess, I'd say she had no friends and only kept people around because they were afraid to leave.

"This is her?" Joan asked. "Doesn't look like much."

I let Rance respond. My job was to get some information and, with any kind of luck, overcome my first impression of the woman.

"Charity is experienced in complex cases, Joan. She can be trusted."

Not a great help there. I guess I was going to have to prove my worth by asking questions and not reacting to her attitude.

"I understand you and Rance think you've been framed for the murder of your... employee."

She snorted. "You can call him my muscle. No need for euphemisms. What are your qualifications? Why should I trust you?"

"I have dealt with a case like yours before," I said. My internal dialog was just a repetition of the word *calm.* "Maybe we should just get down to what I need to know. If when I've finished asking questions you decide I'm not the right person for the job, then no hard feelings."

Joan did that up and down gaze again and then leaned forward. "Okay, we'll try it your way. Just know I'm not a fool. If I don't want to answer your question, you don't push."

That was the worst way to start a case, but she was Rance's problem, not mine. I worked for him, and if I was very lucky this would be my only interaction with her.

"Just don't lie to me. If you won't tell me something I need to know, I'm leaving. I will not take on a case where I'm hamstrung from the get-go."

We engaged in a staring contest long enough for Rance to give an uncomfortable cough to break the tension. I think I got my point across.

"Ask," she said.

"Who would do this to you? Who benefits?"

"There is always some kind of agenda going on in the gang. I might not be as big as some of the other players, but I'm big enough to be a target."

"Okay, but that doesn't answer my question. I'll make it simpler. Who benefits from you being in prison?"

"The two obvious suspects are my second in command and my closest competitor."

"Do you want me to spend time looking up names? The longer this takes, the longer you're out of action. I know Rance will get you bail, but you'll be under observation. You won't be able to run your enterprise, you'll be stuck letting others do the work. Are you looking for a little vacation?"

That made her smile. It didn't soften her at all, just kind of looked like she wanted to bite my head off and suck out my brain. I guess facing someone like Kuznetsov had made me hard to intimidate. I smiled back and waited.

"Fine. My second is Vince Carmichael. I don't think it's him. He likes being ordered around. And the closest competition I have is Jackie Tomasino. He might think it's easier to shut me down in prison than just kill me in a dark alley somewhere."

My experience told me if either of them were behind the frame, then they would have layers of misdirection between them and a cursory investigation. And it was possible that the cops didn't feel compelled to uncover a frame when Joan should already be in prison for any number of other crimes.

"Who else?"

"Isn't figuring that out your job?"

I looked at Rance. He gave me a little smile, like it was all a test. I turned back to Joan.

"Have you pissed anyone off lately? I mean, more than the usual?"

"There may be some cops who aren't happy with me recently. I cut back on some payments. I won't give you names. You need to find that yourself."

Finding corrupt cops was going to be hard and danger-ous. "What was the last job the victim did for you?"

"I won't tell you that," Joan said, in the same tone of voice people on TV used to plead the fifth.

"Okay. Was it a success? Is it possible that the job resulted in his death and someone framing you?"

She opened her mouth to answer and then closed it again. Good, she was thinking. I'd engaged some kind of curiosity, and her abrasiveness might fall away in the pursuit of the answer.

"He was successful. That's why I don't have a motive. Kingston was one of my best."

"Do you think he was killed to frame you, or do you think someone used his death as an opportunity?"

"I have no idea. And I don't see how knowing which came first will help you. It sounds like you plan to find the killer, not the person framing me. Let me deal with whoever killed my man. Just get me free."

There was definitely more to her attitude than a mob boss taking care of business. She didn't seem to think the two events were connected. That someone had taken Kingston's murder as an opportunity to frame her. I'd been working on the idea that someone had killed him for the explicit purpose of setting her up.

"Okay, I have a starting point. I'll probably need to talk to you again sometime. Right now, I only have one last question."

Joan nodded for me to continue.

"When I investigate, I'll dredge up lots of details you might want to keep buried. Is there anything I should know about before I start digging?"

She barked out a laugh and then fixed me with that

dominating gaze again. "Anything you find must be considered client privilege, right?"

I could have pushed but I was worn out by holding my
temper, so I agreed. "I need to talk to Rance before I go."

4

———

"Does she understand that she's in real trouble?" I asked. "You're a great lawyer, but she's going to undermine anything you do to defend her."

"Yes, we have a ways to go to prep her for a trial. If you do your job well, we won't have to worry about that."

Even if I found out it wasn't a frame, Rance had plenty of time to smooth Joan out enough to convince a jury she shouldn't be locked up. Or to treat the people who were trying to help her like they were on her side. "She's on bail, right?"

"Not for the first time. She knows to stick to the rules."

Rance turned to the credenza again, pulling out a file. I got the feeling that he stocked the unit every morning with what he needed, because there was no way it held all his client files; too small, and not at all secure.

"This is what the police sent along. I don't have any discovery from the Crown yet, but we have the bones of the investigation."

"Can I take this away?" I wanted to look over it tonight without Rance standing over me.

"It has to stay here," he said. "You can make notes and take those with you, but the file stays in my office. And no pictures of it either, Charity. I know you hate them, but the rules are there for a reason."

I flipped open the cover and glanced through the few pages. Not much, and some of the copies were difficult to make out. "What could possibly go wrong if I have a copy?"

"Witness tampering, for one. Not you, but someone could get hold of the file who shouldn't."

"Joan seems to think cops are involved. They have access to the originals." She'd tried to pretend she wasn't concerned about the cops on her payroll, but I think that was an act. Interesting that Rance didn't look like he was about to argue the point.

"I'll worry about that when I need to," Rance said. "If you clear her, I don't care so much. If you find the frame came from official sources, that's when it becomes my problem."

"I guess I should get started," I said. I pulled out a notebook, pen, and my phone. I could record some ideas and make physical notes as I went through. "Is there anything in here you think I should focus on?"

He stood and tucked his chair under the table. "I think it's more about what's not there, but I don't want to influence your findings. Call reception when you're ready to go. They'll put the files away."

Glad I didn't have to tell him to leave, I spread my tools out on his desk and started to read.

Six pages didn't take long; Rance had way understated it when he said there were irregularities. I made some notes to ask David, hypothetically, what certain terms meant and what should be in a file like this. I itched to take pictures of the pages despite Rance's warning, but I'd agreed not to.

And copying out by hand or reading aloud didn't feel productive.

I glanced out the window to take in his view of the harbor. The convention center with its pretend-sail roof was buzzing with people coming off cruise ships for an evening in the city. The sky was a perfect blue with streaks of clouds. Like Vancouver was showing off for the visitors.

Rance had a small fridge tucked in the corner behind the couch. Only glass bottles of water inside. I took one, checked again for a snack with no luck. Good thing the file wasn't hundreds of pages long. I was getting hungry and didn't feel like asking someone in reception to get me takeout.

The little break had done its job of clearing my mind. Time to organize my thoughts about the file.

On the inside cover, a sheet listed a directory of documents. Police reports, three witness statements, and Joan's arrest record. It screamed that there was more to find. But maybe the investigators were waiting for more details. It was possible all the details were still in active files and not yet officially received.

I noted the names and addresses of the witnesses. I listed the name of every cop I could find even if they only signed a document as a witness. I added Joan's arrest record. Pretty slim for a crime boss, so probably not the full list. No convictions, in fact no charges. Always some kind of alibi or technical issue that got in the way of putting her in jail. And nothing violent until this murder.

The arrest was based on the witness statements. No gun found at the scene and no evidence like DNA or even fingerprints. Rance brought an interview to a stop when he arrived and Joan must have been smart and waited for him to show before saying a word, so no interrogation on file. It might have helped to see what questions the cops were trying to ask, but nothing got recorded. Suspicious? Maybe not.

This hypothetical case I was building for David looked like it would be bigger than the file. Was that odd? Too many questions.

Rance's comment about what wasn't there piqued my curiosity. I'd seen police files when I worked a handful of cold cases with Leigh. Each one had pictures, autopsy reports, and explanations about leads. None of that was in Joan's documentation. Did someone decide it was Joan and then just arrest her? If that was true, the case would be thrown out of court fast.

Maybe Leigh would be able to get me a copy of the original file. And a picture of the case board, and a rundown of the people involved.

I couldn't quite believe the frame was constructed by cops, and none of the ones I met were this sloppy.

The last items I added to my notes were questions.

If her second in command framed Joan, why now and not earlier? Were there previous attempts?

If her competition did it, again, why now? Did I create a void by taking Kuznetsov down? Why hadn't Rance officially questioned the lack of content in the file? Or had he just not bothered to tell me?

If some cop, or cops, did it, why? My idea of a corrupt cop was one on the payroll of someone like Joan, and she admitted there were some working for her. I couldn't believe this was some kind of vigilante justice thing. That only happened in comic books and Hollywood.

5

———

I made a big salad for dinner with all David's favorite toppings — salmon chunks and fried onions among the most asked for. I needed his advice, and I couldn't ask him outright because of the NDA; as much as it annoyed me, I wasn't planning to break it. My fee didn't rely on my result. If my investigation proved Joan was guilty, I still got paid as long as I got an answer we could rely on in court.

David came home on time, which meant he didn't have an urgent case on the books. If he wasn't busy, he could help me with finding information from the police files. Am I a bad girlfriend because my first thought was how it benefited me? I hadn't made any new friends when I worked with the VPD to catch a killer — well, other than David. So I only had Leigh and my boyfriend to slide me tips and documents.

"I thought you'd be out investigating your new case," he said, before kissing my cheek.

"Go change and I'll have dinner on the table when you get back."

He narrowed his eyes. "You cooked?"

No point in getting offended. I was a lousy cook. "A salad."

He ran up the stairs and a minute later I heard the shower running. I plated the meal and poured us each a glass of pinot grigio while I thought about how to start with my questions.

"How did your meeting go?" David asked when he came back to the living room.

My floating home was tiny, and the area we used most I called the living room, but it was more like an eat-in kitchen where I also worked. There was a closed off room to the rear that we used for watching TV and relaxing. In the summer we mostly relaxed on the roof patio.

"Do you know the client? Rance's, I mean."

"Who it is? Yes, I saw Rance come in when she was arrested. Personally? Well, she's more known to the patrol guys. I did interview her once a couple of years ago. Is she still her own worst enemy?"

I laughed. I figured she'd been aggressively defensive since she was in diapers. "Yep. But my gut tells me she didn't do what she's charged with."

"I'd ask for details, but there's the NDA." He sipped his wine and watched me.

I knew that look. He was waiting for me to tell him how we would get around it. Or, to rail against the injustice of putting any restriction on me.

"You and Leigh are the only people named in that. Do you know why?" I wanted to see him when he told me the answer this time.

"Like I said, protection. If he left us out, the Crown would be able to say you told us everything and then we set up the defense for money. Now, they have to prove you violated the NDA. Unless there's recorded evidence of that, it's impossible."

"Okay, so every question I ask is hypothetical," I said. I cleared the table and brought the wine bottle from the fridge.

"Be careful about what you ask. Keep everything as general as possible."

What I needed right now was questions about procedure, so that was not a problem. "Okay. If I had a client who showed me an arrest report, how thick would it be?"

"Depends. If the case was cut-and-dried, and it was early on, maybe twenty pages. If it was more complicated and longer term, you'd be looking at boxes of evidence."

So, there was a ton of missing paperwork. The thug was murdered three months ago, and they'd only arrested Joan this week.

"What kind of documents?"

"You saw the files the last time you worked with us. Investigator notes, witness statements, transcripts of suspect interviews, photos, autopsy report, arrest warrant documentation, names and addresses of anyone interviewed. Theories too, but they would be sketchy. Mostly used to prove the investigation didn't narrow down too fast, like they chose their perp and only looked for evidence to prove they were right."

"Does that happen?" The size of Joan's file made me suspect the investigation did exactly that.

"Not these days," David said. "Too many cases get thrown out. Professional Standards audits our work randomly. It's not worth risking a career because the odds are you'll get caught."

Professional Standards was the VPD equivalent to Internal Investigations. In reality cops didn't treat them the way you see on TV, but no one likes being accused of wrong-doing, so the relationship wasn't cordial.

If what he said was true and not just a rule that got ignored a lot, the paperwork was probably somewhere. "Does Professional Standards check to see what's been sent to the defense lawyer? Or the Crown?"

"Hypothetically?"

I nodded.

"Not unless either lawyer asks. If you think we sent an incomplete file, you should call it in."

If someone reported a problem, it would need to be Rance. He knew more than I did about the process. And maybe he was waiting for me to find the proof before using the leverage.

"I didn't say that it was even hypothetically possible. I just can't remember the details from the Hargreaves case."

He let that sit for a minute. I didn't know if he was trying to think about what he could tell me or decide if I was lying to him for a good reason. I kept quiet because I wasn't technically lying. I didn't remember, but those cases had been completely different from the investigation I really wanted to solve, so I hadn't really paid much attention.

"Okay, what else? Hypothetically?"

"Who signs the forms like the arrest, or the complaint?"

"The complaint could be anyone who took the call. The arrest forms get signed by the detective and the sergeant."

There were no ranks on the documents I'd seen. I couldn't get into the names because there was no hypothetical in that level of detail. I'd ask Leigh when we got together.

"Any advice?" It would help to know what the official investigators would do.

"Look for motive. It's not where we usually start. But

when it's a crime that might involve internal gang violence, we start with who might benefit the most from putting the boss away."

"I wasn't planning on taking the client's word for anything, but that might help."

"Are we done? There's a game on in a half hour."

I wanted one solid clue, and it was hard when I had to skirt around the questions. "How do I talk to the people who signed the documents?" Maybe it would be that easy.

"Their contact information, rank, and full name should be on the document; if not, there's a separate form with all that."

6

———

Leigh handed her menu to the server and then gave me one of those 'I know you want something' stares.

No point in playing games. She was a friend. More than that — she'd saved my life at least twice. "I need to pick your brain," I said.

She added a couple packs of sugar to her coffee. "On the Tiller case?"

How did she know? David told me it would be public record, but he never said the client's name. Maybe to keep our hypothetical game running?

"I can't confirm that," I said. "But what do you know?"

"Rance hired you to find a way to get her off the murder charge." She sounded pissed, and that was new.

"I signed an NDA, but say that was true — if she's innocent, she should go free."

"She's not innocent."

I couldn't argue. Joan ran a criminal organization, no way could she claim innocence. But that didn't mean she deserved to be framed for a crime she didn't commit. "Of this particular crime? Or in general?"

The server placed our plates on the table. Bacon, eggs, and toast for me, oatmeal and fruit for Leigh. As soon as we started eating, the woman would be back asking if the food was okay. I took a bite and didn't push for an answer until we were left alone in peace. The buzz of conversation at the tables around us provided a bit of cover. Unless someone really concentrated on us, we wouldn't be overheard. That didn't help my paranoia. I felt watched. I looked around and there were no uniformed cops or detectives I recognized in the restaurant, so I tried to relax.

Leigh mixed the fruit into her bowl and waited too. I think I saw a touch of regret on her face for her last words, but maybe I just hoped it was regret and not annoyance at me.

When we were sure of privacy, Leigh said, "I don't know about this crime. If she didn't do it, she shouldn't be charged. Maybe she didn't pull the trigger, but just ordered a hit."

What I'd seen in the files didn't lead to that conclusion. "No one else was charged," I said. "I don't know that anyone else was properly investigated. How would I know if that was true?"

Leigh thought that over while she finished her healthy meal. I tried to talk myself out of suspicion that she'd changed. Until now, she was a straight cop. She'd been promoted to detective, and when we worked the cold cases, she'd been careful to follow the rules. This suspicion could be all from me. I didn't have a stellar history with the VPD and trust.

She finally came to her conclusion and started talking. "The file should contain the details. I'm surprised Rance hasn't given you copies of everything that was sent. What exactly was there?"

Given me? Add Rance to the list of people I couldn't trust completely. "I can't get specific. I've seen the file he received. It's thin. I don't think that's right, do you? I know you can look it up if you want, but I can't break the NDA, at least not this early in the case. What would I look for in a file to show the investigators looked at other suspects?"

She pushed her bowl aside and stared at me. "It should be thick with all her priors. That woman keeps getting away with crimes, but the paperwork still remains even if she skips on the charge. What's in there?" She shook her head and held up her hand to stop me. "I know, you can't talk about it."

"I'm pretty sure someone edited the documents Rance got. A lot of the information David said should be there wasn't."

She drank the last of her coffee as she thought that over. I let her have the time while I ate my bacon and eggs.

The table cleared and our coffees topped up, Leigh took a deep breath before saying, "If that's true, then someone is risking their career. If she was framed, it wouldn't be worth that for a cop. It will be someone in her organization, or a rival. Or there would be a lot more going on than killing a gang enforcer."

I agreed with her, but the few leads I had were pointing to someone at VPD working for Joan. Her statement and the police file and my gut. "I need to see the official file," I said. "The one that has all the notes and history."

"I can't get it for you," she said. "Charity, I can't interfere. If a cop is involved, I can't risk the Professional Standards people linking me to the case. David can't either."

"It was worth a try," I said. "I hope it's just one cop on her payroll, or someone at Rance's office. Whoever received the file could have pulled documents, right? I'll find another way."

"Get Rance to do it. He has a right to question the credibility of the evidence sent. And he needs to know for sure if the investigation was focused only on Tiller. I'm not saying they should have done it, but there has to be a reason she was the only suspect. *If* she was. Don't forget that without the evidence, this is all guesswork."

I would talk to Rance as a last resort. He wanted me to find the proof and I needed to do that for him, or at least give it a good try. "If I can't get what I need any other way, I'll do that."

She leaned forward and spoke quietly. "Rance would know what should be there. Maybe you're looking in the wrong place for your corruption."

I'd thought of that. If Rance knew the file was short, then was he testing me? What was I supposed to do with that? Exactly what I was doing. Work the case I was given and find him answers. There was no smart reason he would manipulate me like that.

"So much for an easy case," I said.

"You didn't think for a minute it would be easy," Leigh said. "I'll help where I can, Charity, and so will David, you know that. I won't risk the court case, or my career to help you, but if you find out there's a conspiracy at our end, I won't cover up for them either."

7

We got back to Leigh's desk, and I grabbed the jacket I'd left there as an excuse to come back inside the VPD station. At the time, I'd hoped Leigh would slip me some details, or have the case file open on her computer. Since that was a no, I grabbed my jacket and turned to go.

"You're that Deacon PI," a woman said behind me. I turned to see a blond a bit shorter than me who clearly lifted weights. Beside her was a tall, skinny Black cop who looked like he was fresh from the academy.

"Yes," I said, like I'd missed the sneer in her voice. "Can I help you?"

"You should stick to taking sleazy pictures," the guy said. "Stay out of police cases."

Behind them, Leigh was returning from the washroom. I figured I could play this out a bit so she could get in on the action.

"Is that the official stance?"

"It's close enough," the woman said. "You should listen."

Or else what? Neither wore name badges, but Leigh

would know them. If they thought I'd be scared off, they were completely wrong. Okay, not completely. My body tingled with adrenaline, not sure if this was a fight or flight situation— or from fear of getting on the wrong side of the patrol cops. Now was the time for bravado, though. And I had Leigh on my side — or, when she got to her desk I would.

"I'll wait until I hear officially, thanks." I tried to make my voice as neutral as possible.

"You might change your mind," the guy said.

If these two were part of the conspiracy against Joan, they were pretty stupid. Maybe they didn't like PIs. Or, maybe they were just assholes. I still thought cops were involved, but if it was these two, I'd be shocked. With that kind of ham-handedness, they would have been caught the first time they tried something.

"What's going on here?" Leigh asked.

"Nothing, just talking," the woman said.

Both turned to walk away like nothing happened, but Leigh stood in their path. "Where are your name badges?" she asked.

Both reached for where the tags should have been on their uniform shirts. "Must have left it in my locker," the woman said.

The guy lifted his chin like Leigh was beneath his worth.

"Then get them and go back to work," she said. "This floor is for detectives." She stood aside and watched until they stepped into the elevator.

"Badass," I said. "Is that true? That they shouldn't be up here?"

She shrugged. "Not really. I mean, we can't have just anyone hanging around with ongoing investigations displayed in the murder rooms. They didn't have any business up here, so yeah."

"Do you know who they were?"

"What did they say to you?" she asked. "I saw your face, I know it wasn't good, so don't say nothing."

"Clumsy threats. I don't know if it was about the Tiller case, or just general dislike of me or my profession."

"You can make a complaint," she said. "I mean, I used to be in uniform. If they're going to threaten someone, they should be better at it than that."

I laughed at the idea of training for intimidating civilians.

"No. It's real," Leigh said. "Sometimes we have to come down hard and training keeps us on the right side of the line. Doing it wrong can blow a case."

"I don't want to get involved with Professional Standards, but I do want to know who they are." A complaint would mean an investigation, and I didn't want anything getting in the way of my case. "Just be nice to know their names."

"Lucy Valette and Bill Walker. I've never been on a case with them, but I like to know who's working here."

Two names from the case file. Maybe I was wrong to dismiss them. A clumsy threat might be just the first shot in a campaign to discredit me. "I'll let you know if I start getting pulled over for driving while being a PI."

"I don't think they'll risk it," she said. "They're just assholes. Sad to say the screening doesn't always sift out the kind of personality that gets a high from wielding power."

I wasn't so sure, but nothing had happened so far to give me any sense that Leigh was wrong. "Okay. I'll let you get back to work. I'll find another way to get a lead."

"I'm sorry I can't help with the Tiller case, Charity. I will look into Valette and Walker, though. Just in case, you know."

"I didn't mean it that way. I get you can't always bend the rules without repercussions." I appreciated the help she did give me, and I suspected that by looking into them she'd be helping me with Joan's case, anyway.

I wasn't quite on my own yet. Matthieu might not be coming back to work, but he could hand out some advice. I wasn't sure how I managed to solve anything back when I worked solo. We didn't generally work the same cases, but we were each other's backup. I was used to giving and getting updates until he left for France. I'm not sure whether the new way of working was better, or worse, or just different.

I headed out to my car, planning to make the trip to North Van before I settled in at home or Rance's office. Maybe baby Theo would be napping, and we could chat. If not, I didn't mind getting a cuddle or two in while Matthieu talked.

My phone pinged just before I got to my car. A text from Paul Grewal. *Call me.* He'd done his best to keep me from tying our cold cases to his hot one when I worked with Leigh. He did soften to me at the end, but only when it was obvious I was right. I put my phone in my pocket. Whatever he wanted could wait. I wasn't in the mood to do battle with him or any other cop today.

8

On the way to Lu's, I called Rance and made an appointment for later. Since my usual sources wouldn't be able to get me the original case documents, I might have to ask him to check that he received everything. And asking would give me an opportunity to assess his reaction. Unless the investigation was sloppy and rushed, he should have noticed a problem when the file was received.

Lu opened the front door before I had a chance to knock.

"Quiet, please. Theo just fell asleep."

"I don't plan to shout, or burst balloons," I said as I followed her through to the back patio. The heaters were on and Matthieu was sitting at a wrought iron cafe-style table in a matching chair. The baby monitor rested in the center, a glass of wine on a cork pad and a plate of sandwiches to the side.

"I'll get you a glass," Lu whispered.

"I can't stay long, just some water would be great, and I can get it."

She nudged me toward the table. "You can talk to Matthieu and grab a sandwich."

"Afternoon, Charity," Matthieu said in a normal voice.

"What happened to 'be quiet'?" I asked. The aroma of grilled peppers, zucchini, olive oil, and herbs de Provence reached me. I took half a sandwich and used a napkin for a plate.

"Lu is more cautious," he said. "It is fair because she is more affected by his cries. I simply lose sleep."

I didn't want to know the details of her reaction to baby tears. "Do you have a few minutes? I need some advice."

"Of course. It keeps my hand in, as you say. What do you need?"

Lu joined us, placing a large glass of iced tea beside my sandwich. "Oh, good. It's been too long since you talked to me about a case."

The fact that they'd been in France for almost a year made it hard to have cozy chats, but I didn't care. It felt like normal times to sit here.

I gave them a rundown of my thoughts; the case was looking like a frame, but I hadn't talked to any potential suspects. The cops, the NDA, the file. And my worries about police involvement.

Matthieu nodded as I spoke and then paused before giving me his thoughts. Lu pushed me to eat, and I told her she was looking too skinny. We ate and drank and enjoyed the view of Vancouver until Matthieu sat forward.

"I cannot be sure without meeting this client, or reading the documentation," he said. "But if you are being threatened, there is a reason. If there is corruption, it will be very hard to prove, and perhaps not your job."

He'd quit the Gendarmerie because he was tired of no one dealing with the corruption in his office. Although, I'm pretty sure he would still be there if he hadn't fallen in love with my best friend.

"I can't just go to Professional Standards and leave a general complaint," I said. "It won't go anywhere, and my client will still be looking at a trial."

"You remember Colonel Fitzroi?" he asked.

How could I forget? We couldn't prove anything, and he told us he was part of an undercover operation, but I'd bet my left arm that he was working for the Russian gangs who smuggled anything and everything through his town. "Hard to forget."

"He has disappeared. First, he retired, I hear it was to avoid charges. Then we find he is gone, not spending his pension, not traveling under his name. Nothing. I believe he has been eliminated by his former partners."

"Or, they gave him a new identity and plenty of money," I said. "Unless you have proof, I don't see why we assume they killed him. Too risky. He might be a bad cop, but he's still a cop, and if the body is found, the investigation won't stop, right?"

"If he was killed," Matthieu said, "then no one would find a body, Charity. But yes, we have not even a tiny hint of a clue. So, we do not know."

I thought back to my own experience with international gangs and couldn't really argue that Fitzroi wasn't at the bottom of the Mediterranean, but I kept the argument to myself. It was history, and I had a current case to solve. Although Fitzroi had made a stab at convincing us he wasn't dirty. "So he was corrupt?"

"Yes. There are some outstanding charges, but no one expects to see him again," Matthieu said. "We all know he was complicit in Audrey Wylie's kidnapping. None of us believed the story that he was undercover."

"So, you're saying if he got away with it, I don't have a chance," I said. "I have to hope I find the source of the frame-up within her associates and adversaries."

"It will be dangerous," he said. "You must keep Rance aware of your suspicions. And David, at least. It will be allowed within your NDA. And remember, your client is Rance, not Madame Tiller. He wants the truth, not a complicated conspiracy that cannot help her."

Lu gave him a playful jab. "You sound like you think she should drop the case. Charity can take care of herself."

I wasn't so sure I wanted to take care of myself again. I mean, at some point my luck was going to run out, and the last two cases had taken a lot of it. But I wasn't a quitter, and I couldn't afford to drop the case. "I don't have enough to point fingers. If I do, I'll pass my evidence along to Rance and David as soon as I can. I'll make a report and walk away."

"I hope so," Matthieu said. "But my lovely wife is right, you have always managed to survive."

I gave him a kiss on the cheek in farewell and followed Lu to take a peek at the sleeping baby.

"He's beautiful," I said. All babies are, but this one was special.

"Even when he's bawling and fussy, I think that," she said.

"I have an appointment with Rance in a bit," I said. "Thanks for letting me talk it through."

"Any time. I meant what I said. You can handle this. But if it turns out that this woman is being framed by someone in authority, you are only one person. Ask for help before the last second this time, please."

"It may not be," I said. "My gut is saying that Joan is being framed. But there are lots of players. And someone interfered with the case documents. So at least one cop is involved. I promise I'll go looking at the cops last, not first."

9

R ance was waiting for me in the lobby of the building when I walked in. "Have you eaten?" he asked.

"I'm good. I don't think this will take long." I didn't want to spend my time waiting for food to arrive, and I hoped David would be home tonight so we could eat together — and maybe so he could answer a few more questions about a hypothetical client. I didn't tell Rance that; he didn't need to know anything about my private life.

We settled in his office at the couch and comfyish chairs, coffees on the table in front of us and my back to the view. Not some power play on his part. I chose the seat because I wanted to concentrate. I pulled out my notepad and gave him a report on my lack of progress.

"The first phase is getting grounded," I said. "This is a different case from my usual, and I don't want to create problems just because I ask the wrong question at the wrong time."

"How long do you think the first phase will last?" He

sounded interested, not annoyed. A good lawyer probably had expert level skills in hiding emotions.

"I'll start talking to Joan's people and her rival tomorrow. So, I guess it's over after this meeting."

He gestured for me to continue.

"I think we have some cops involved," I said. "I don't know how deep, or how tightly controlled, but Joan told me she has some on her payroll. That means her second might have some, and her rival definitely does."

"I wouldn't trust Joan's word," he said. "I'm not saying she isn't paying off a few officers to turn a blind eye, but her organization isn't big enough to do more than that."

"I get that, but this is her freedom she's risking. You don't think she's motivated to tell the truth?"

"There is always some agenda with her. Not just her; career criminals in general are pulling multiple strings all the time. They think it's all in control, but it doesn't take much to unravel their plans."

If Joan lied to me, I wouldn't be able to help her; but Rance knew her and her type better than I did. My connection with the criminal world was mostly limited to petty insurance fraud and a little light embezzlement. Okay, when it wasn't serial murderers, or people traffickers, or Russian mob bosses.

"I'll keep it in mind. I got a bit of hassle at the VPD station when I went to talk to Leigh Andrews." No point in pretending I was steering clear of the two people named in the NDA. I gave him the details and he asked for the names.

"Probably just needed to feel powerful," Rance said. "I'll do a bit of discreet checking for you."

Help like that was the last thing I needed. "That might make things worse," I said. "I'll ask if I need you."

"What else?"

I liked that he didn't argue with me. I should probably ask about the case file, but my gut was whispering that it wasn't the right time. Since his first instinct was to interfere — I mean help — I needed more proof, or at least one piece of proof that the file was missing documentation, and not just the result of a piss poor job on behalf of the investigation team. "The NDA. Everyone seems to know about it. Not talking about things with my two best resources is dragging the case out. I don't want to slip up."

He grinned like the whole secrecy thing was a joke. "I can't believe you haven't signed one before. When you worked with the VPD, or the RCMP?"

"But everyone I needed was inside the walls. This time I'm cut off." I tried for a joking tone to cover what I knew would sound like a whine. Not sure I succeeded. "What happens if I need help?"

"It should be pretty straightforward, Charity. You can't share specifics of what you found. Anything available to the public without the help of a hacker is open for discussion. If you're worried, we can have your resources sign NDAs."

That would keep me running back for paperwork. Rance knew it wasn't a valid option. I hadn't replaced my best source of information, Guy, but there were a few people on the edge of the criminal world who I trusted, and who might have information. And none of them would sign a document that would prove they'd helped me.

"I was kidding. I know, your sources won't sign an NDA, or won't do it in good faith," Rance said. "The cops can't sign one because they need to be free of outside influence. But they'll find a way around it. Just go carefully. Remember that whatever you find needs to convince a judge to vacate the charges and the police to do a real investigation."

I heard him encouraging me to bend the agreement

right up to the breaking point. "I'll need to interview Joan again before I start following up on leads. How soon can we make that happen?"

He picked up his phone and checked his schedule. "She violated her bail conditions, so you'll do that at the jail. You want me to make sure she doesn't piss you off enough to resign the case?"

She must have ended up in jail on purpose. Joan knew the system too well to accidentally break bail. "I'll be fine. I'm probably more stubborn than she is aggressive."

"Anything else?"

"I need to look closer at the files," I said. "Not just the police file, but your notes and strategies, and anything you have on Joan and her organization. And her rivals, and maybe the arrest reports for her previous crimes."

"That will take some time," he said. "Do you want hard copies, or would cloud access work?"

That meant I could go home and review documents with a glass of wine and a pizza. And if David peeked over my shoulder, maybe that would be okay. "Cloud would be better. That way you can add things as you get them, and I'll have them right away."

He made a note to give me access and I headed out. It was early enough that I could make the trip to the jail and still be home in time for dinner.

10

The man in charge of jail visitation tried to stop me from talking to Joan. He could easily have succeeded; I wasn't a lawyer or a doctor so I couldn't demand to see her. I didn't do my usual shtick of pretend threats and sarcasm. I wanted this over with. I called Rance, he talked to the cop. I got in.

The room was the definition of bleak. I'd been here before, but usually in the presence of cops, so I had other things to focus on. Now, alone while I waited for Joan to show up, all I could do was feel the despair. The chairs were metal and bolted to the floor; the table matched and had a bar across the center for handcuffs. The floor was concrete, with a fair number of mystery stains and three large cracks spidering to the gray walls. The ceiling was flat panels with random holes and a giant water stain.

Joan walked in, followed by a guard who went and stood in the corner. She wasn't cuffed, and acted like he was her manservant. I ignored the act.

"I have a few questions," I said. If she was going to be a demanding bitch, then I was getting what I needed and leaving ASAP. I had people to talk to and a case to solve. My job here was to get answers, and my hope was they would be enough to let me find the person framing her, so I'd never have to talk to her again.

"Why else would I be here? I appreciate the field trip from my cell, but I have business to conduct." Joan slid her eyes from mine just long enough to check what the guard was doing. "Just me and her," Joan said. "I don't want you knowing anything about my business."

He reached for the radio on his shoulder and relayed Joan's request. The answer came back in her favor and the guard looked like he was going to object. Joan stared at him and he left. To stand outside the door, I'm pretty sure, or to watch the video of our meeting. I looked at the camera in the corner at that thought. No lights on. We weren't being recorded.

I turned to Joan. "We're alone. Are you ready to answer questions now? And not just a list of names. You don't know who's framing you, so it could be someone you haven't thought of."

She leaned forward to avoid raising her voice. "I don't want anyone knowing my business. I get that you need information, but I can't trust anyone with all of it. I'll do my best, but if details get out, you'll be on my list to be dealt with."

I heard the threat. She wasn't talking about suing me. Dealing with me would require a gun and a disposal site. Good thing I'd been threatened before.

"I signed an NDA, and I don't have to tell Rance anything more than my results. Are you planning on telling me about a murder you're arranging?"

"No."

"Then we're good. My job is to find out if you are being framed." I didn't get a chance to continue.

"I am. That you can rely on. I had no reason to get rid of Kingston."

"Don't interrupt me," I said. Inside, I was trembling, but I couldn't let her think she had me under control. "I was about to say that I agree. Even without the details, it's obvious something is wrong with the case."

I wasn't going to tell her about the police file, or anything really. This was about her giving me answers, not an exchange of information.

My tone must have amused her because she smiled and relaxed back in her chair. The smile might have been meant to reassure me, but it looked more like the expression a snake gets when it has a mouse in sight.

"Ask away," she said with a wave of her hand.

"You gave me names; I want to know why each of them would want to frame you. I don't want the usual stuff; I can use my imagination. I need real motives."

"Smart. First of all, just a general statement, none of those people have a strong motive. I'm not saying don't look into that, but if I thought any of them were attempting to take over, I'd... Oh, I shouldn't confess to planning a crime."

"Fine, so why would your second in command, Vince, kill Kingston if not to take over?" I pulled out my own notepad and pen.

"Killing Kingston might not be the end goal," Joan said. "Taking me out of the picture is the only way to take over."

"Yes, I know that. But what if framing you was just a way to avoid being arrested for the murder? A bonus, if you like."

That surprised her. I gave myself a mental gold star for considering something she hadn't.

"I don't like to think I'm just a side effect. But Vince sent

Kingston on... an errand he didn't complete. So, maybe he was killed as an example."

"What was the errand?"

"Nothing to do with your job."

"The less you tell me the harder it's going to be to solve the case, and the longer you'll be in jail." I looked closely at her expression. Nothing. It might just be the environment, but I didn't like not being able to read her emotions. "Was it a big problem? Was Kingston prone to failing?"

"A bigger problem for Vince if he failed. He needs to keep up a reputation. Minor for my operation. Kingston was good at his job, but this errand was new for him."

That gave me all kinds of questions to ask Vince when we met. "And Jackie Tomasino? Could he be trying to take over your business?"

"We were in discussions about a merger. He could be getting impatient, but me in jail just delays everything."

"Kingston's errand, was it anything to do with Jackie?"

"No."

"Had Jackie run up against Kingston in the past?"

"Not as far as I know," Joan said. Her answer was too fast for me to trust her. She was holding something back, but I'd try to get the details from Jackie.

"Police?" I said. I let the question sit there. She'd told me that she'd cut the income for some cops on her payroll, but not how much. Maybe enough to push them from taking bribes to killing.

She crossed her arms and leaned back in her chair. "I won't give you names unless you can prove they are involved."

"What was your relationship with Kingston? Maybe someone killed him to punish you?"

"We slept together occasionally. Nothing that would give

him any leverage over me. I'm very careful about that kind of thing. And he's easy to replace, so no one killed him to damage my organization."

On the way out, I got hassled again about visiting hours. Someone here didn't like me. That might have nothing to do with Joan, though.

11

At home I opened a new file and started my plan. I'd eaten up too much time trying to get my head around the assignment. Proving Joan was framed shouldn't be that hard, but she could have just pissed someone off enough in one encounter to start a whole chain of events that led her to a murder charge and Rance's office. It occurred to me that in the criminal world, there was always someone who would want to expand. Vancouver, like any port city, was attractive to all kinds of criminals, along with regular citizens wanting a sea view. Legitimate business brought us a steady flow of things we wanted and needed, along with smuggled drugs, weapons, and people.

Apparently Rance didn't think to mention screenshots being forbidden, but the read-only setting he had on his documents didn't let me take any. I tried taking a photo of the screen with my phone, but too much reflection and a less than steady hand didn't give me a legible copy. Even if I'd bought the tripod I kept promising myself, the print was too small to be of use in a picture. Enlarging it just gave me blurry pixels. The man was smart.

I made a couple of pages of notes from previous arrest records. Names of cops, names of witnesses, names of people who gave Joan alibis, and the names I had to follow up on. Rance's files weren't exactly flush with information, but they contained more than the police file. I guess it was too much to expect that I'd get his notes on Joan through the years.

What surprised me the most was how excited I was with this criminal case. I'd sworn to go back to safe and boring clients as soon as I finished consulting with the RCMP. That lasted just over a week. Maybe I should embrace my inner adrenaline junkie and stop pretending I liked insurance claim fraud.

I thought back to the original conversation with Rance. He wanted me to prove the frame; I'd been working on the assumption that I would only prove it by catching the person who framed her, or the real killer. I liked the idea of pulling a killer off the streets, and I had no idea how to prove the frame without finding whoever ended Kingston's life. If Joan had an alibi, or some other way to show she was innocent — at least of this murder — then I wouldn't be working on the case.

I stared at the screen. Letting my thoughts spin in circles wasn't helping me as much as it usually did. The atmosphere was right — quiet with only the occasional seagull scream to break the peace. I hoped it was just a phase of the investigation, not that I'd lost my mojo. I loved being a PI and couldn't imagine any other way to pay the bills.

I had no one to call for criminal gossip. I missed Guy, and not just because he was a great source, but because I kind of liked him. I didn't miss him enough to disobey the order to drop him from the boss of the local Angels chapter.

It wasn't all bad; I had names of people to interview. I had two cops who were pissed with me for some reason. That wasn't a new situation. I did have some friends in the department — okay, I had Leigh and David. But most cops were suspicious of civilians poking into crime. I got the feeling that they would be happy for us PIs to stay with civil cases. They didn't like us considering ourselves professionals.

Another drift away from the problem in front of me. I straightened in my chair, took a sip of my coffee, and started typing. The names went down in order of likelihood they'd have something helpful. Starting with Vince, Joan's second in command, and ending with a question mark. Did Kingston have any enemies I didn't know about? This could be as simple as someone taking advantage of a situation to frame Joan and get her out of the business.

I thought about the times I'd worked with cops. They would look for motive and opportunity. Maybe they wouldn't consider framing Joan a serious crime. But I did. So, was there anyone with a motive to either kill Kingston or frame Joan? Everyone on the list so far, and some unnamed cops. And maybe a new player in the market. The list didn't help yet, but keeping things on record meant I wouldn't lose an idea later.

The door opened and I closed the lid for my laptop. David walked in, followed by Paul Grewal.

12

"What is he doing here?" I didn't feel like being polite or welcoming to someone I had been ignoring. There was a very fine line between persistence and stalking.

"Just listen to him," David said. "I know you don't want to, but do it for me."

I sat back in my chair and crossed my arms tightly to make sure he got the message. "Start talking."

Paul pulled out a chair opposite and sat. "I think you need help with your case."

I let it go because it would be petty to tell him I hadn't invited him to sit, and I didn't want David to think I was quite so petty. I nodded for him to continue. I mean, if he was really about to help me out, I guess I could overlook the way he treated me when I worked the Hargreaves case.

"I heard what happened." He paused for me to start talking.

I didn't give him any hint that I knew what he was talking about.

"At the station."

He might have a better idea what was behind the nasty comments. "And?"

"I hate that attitude, and I hate dirty cops."

That encounter didn't rise to the level of dirty cops. "You think the frame-up is coming from your buddies?"

"Charity," David said, sounding disappointed, which hurt.

"Not my buddies," Paul said. "Look, I know I was an asshole to you at the start of the cold cases, but it wasn't personal. I didn't know how good you were. I just thought you'd screw things up."

Fair enough. Our only connection at that time was Leigh, and she had been new to Homicide and proving herself. I met David on that case. And while I begrudged any acknowledgment of his help, Paul did get on board at the end — when the whole thing was neatly wrapped up.

"I can handle a couple of patrol officers with fragile egos," I said.

"Constables, Charity," David said.

Now he was getting annoyed at me. Okay, maybe I was pushing the attitude too much. "What's your proposal?"

"The Joan Tiller case. To be clear, I can help you with the idiots from the station too, but I think someone is inter-fering with her case. I don't know if she's the killer, but the whole investigation seems off, and I want whoever actually killed the guy to spend years in prison — not just some convenient criminal scapegoat."

"Can you get me the original case file?" I knew he couldn't. The original would stay in records, but a copy would be good.

"Then you'll let me help?"

"I can't," I said. "I signed an NDA and Rance will shut me down if I tell you any details."

"We can deal with that," Paul said. "I'll use personal days, so I won't be on active duty while we work together."

"I'll think about it." I really wanted that file, and I was pretty sure Rance would be okay with me getting Paul's help.

"You think the file we sent to Rance has things missing?"

His question brought a thought to my mind. "I'm wondering if the file sent to the Crown is the same."

"That I can find out for you," Paul said. "Look, I get that you can't just say yes, but if there's corruption to the point that cops are framing people, that's a huge problem. I'll check the files for you while you think it over."

13

"**Y**ou should work with him," David said when we were alone. "You need a partner."

I opened my laptop again to stall. I wasn't mad at him. But I wasn't happy, either. He was interfering, and I thought we had an agreement about that. He should have talked to me first. That thought gave me a twinge. Maybe he'd tried and I hadn't listened. Maybe I should have talked to Paul, and not just ignored him until he was forced to use David to get to me.

I couldn't get my thoughts together and I couldn't stall with silence much longer. David was patient, but not a saint. "I need to make a call."

He nodded and headed upstairs. I had the time it would take for him to shower to come up with an answer we could both live with.

I hit the phone number Joan gave me for Vince, her second in command. I hoped she'd told him to cooperate — and that he wasn't the culprit.

"Yeah?" A gravelly voice barked. He sounded like he'd been smoking cheap cigars for fifty years.

I introduced myself and asked if we could meet tonight. I knew I was looking for a way to avoid talking with David about Paul, but I did have to interview Vince.

"Busy tonight," he rasped. "Not sure when I can find the time."

He moved up my list of potential framers. The only reason to deny me access was that he had a secret. "Did Joan call you?"

"Yeah. Said I should help. But to be clear, I won't give you anything that damages the gang."

He wasn't planning on making this easy. Fine, I had some unresolved feelings to take out on someone. "Should I tell her you refused? I can make the call right now."

There was a long pause, and finally he grunted and said, "She wants the business to keep running and that usually takes two of us. She won't let me use one of our guys to help and now she expects me to talk to someone we'd usually tell to fuck off."

I guess I wasn't the only one with a load of pissed-off to pass on. "Okay, I'll make it fast. I'm not doing this on the phone. I can't assure Joan you're innocent until we talk face-to-face. You don't want to be the last person I talk to. Joan doesn't seem like the patient or understanding type. Make time tomorrow, or she might question your loyalty."

Another long pause. The sound of the shower stopped upstairs, so David would be back in a few minutes. I wanted to poke Vince harder, but it might shove him in the wrong direction. He could hang up rather than concede.

"Okay, eleven tomorrow morning. I'll text you the details."

"Just you, no henchmen. No tricks."

"Yeah, yeah." He ended the call.

David wrapped me in a hug. He smelled of shampoo

and lemon soap. I couldn't stay annoyed with him when all I wanted to do was snuggle.

"Ready to talk?" he asked.

I entered the appointment with Vince in my calendar and then closed my laptop. I wasn't ready to talk, but I figured I would never be, so this was as good a time as any. "Why should I trust Paul?"

He grinned and poured me a glass of pinot grigio. "I don't know if you should, completely. He gets territorial, you've seen that, but he's a good cop."

It helped that he didn't try to sell me on blindly joining forces with Paul. "Is there something I should know?"

He leaned against the kitchen counter and sipped at his wine. "There is, but it's his story. You need help, right? And I can't do anything for you without jeopardizing the case. Anything I give you will be suspicious. Paul has contacts just like I do, Charity."

I really missed Guy again. Not that he would be able to get me files from the police station, but because he would know about cops on the take. "How is he going to help if he takes time off?"

"He can still get into the station, still access databases, still talk to his friends." He put his glass on the counter and grabbed his phone. "I'm hungry. Pizza?"

He knew how to stall me. I nodded and tucked my laptop in my bag. I'd go back to my investigation plan later. This conversation was too important for me to be distracted. "Are you one of his friends? Is this a way for you to help me?"

"Possibly, but Paul has a big reach in the department. He's been around for way longer than me." He finished ordering dinner and put his phone to the side. "You've worked with people you don't like before, right? What's the worst that could happen?"

The only time I'd worked with someone I didn't trust, it was Paul Grewal. I was going to have to decide blindly on this one. He was a good cop, and he did give me credit at the end of the case. Maybe his asshole behavior before I proved the cases were connected was just territorial protection. "It's going to be up to Rance in the end," I said. "I'll talk to Paul again before I ask for permission."

"I'll set it up for later," David said. "Coffee at the Bayshore?"

I kind of liked having an assistant. I checked the time on my phone. It was just before seven. "Ten, I'll get decaf or tea so I can sleep."

He sent the text and two responses pinged back. "Pizza is on its way. Paul says he'll be there."

David headed to the security gate to wait for the food. I grabbed plates and napkins and put the remaining wine in our glasses. My phone rang just as I finished.

I didn't recognize the number but answered anyway. "Deacon Investigations."

"Let the system deal with Joan Tiller." It was a woman, or some voice distorting software making it sound female. Low and crisp, the words carried no emotion, which felt more like a threat than shouting.

"I have a job to do," I said. I must have made progress if someone felt the need to threaten me.

"The world will be better with Tiller inside."

If only that was the way things worked. "Maybe, but she should go down for something she did, not just a convenient crime."

"If you don't let it go, someone might decide the world would be better off without you, too."

The call ended before I could respond. David opened the door and brought the warm smell of pizza sauce and melted cheese inside. I was not going to spoil dinner by telling him about the call.

14

The marina I lived in was quiet, but between me and the coffee shop was a popular restaurant. It did great takeout, and was a favorite of the night-out and cocktails crowds.

I dodged some waiting taxis and Ubers, then headed through the hotel lobby to meet Paul. In the time since the pizza arrived, I'd come to the conclusion that I did need Paul's help. But I wasn't the one who would make the final decision. Rance could say no and that would be it. I mean, I could still use Paul, but not as a partner, and this case was tricky enough that I needed one of those.

He was sitting at a table stuck in the far corner of the space. Two chairs, his coffee, and a chai for me. No, he didn't know me that well; I'd sent him my order when I was through the security gate. No one sat nearby. We would be as private as possible in a public space.

I tossed my jacket on the back of the empty chair and sat. I wasn't planning any power games, but I still couldn't get myself to start the conversation by simply agreeing to take him on.

"Thanks for coming," he said. "And for not just telling me to piss off."

"Were you expecting payback?" I had considered it, but I wasn't as territorial as he was.

"Maybe a little. I'm sorry I didn't give you a chance before. It's just so rare we ask a civilian to help and they actually do."

"I did more than help." I couldn't stop myself from saying the words. I guess I was holding on to more resentment about the Hargreaves case than I thought.

"Yes, you and Leigh figured out that the cases were all connected. You caught the killer. We did nothing, right?"

I laughed. His apology skills might need a tweak. Of course, so could mine.

"Okay, truce. You know what my last couple of cases were, so you must know I'm competent. The Hargreaves case wasn't a fluke."

"Truce." He held out his hand for a shake. "Just cut me some slack. I'm not as used to investigations that don't run with rules as you are."

I was pretty sure his definition of rules was stricter than mine. "We will work within the official guidelines as much as possible. Rance needs this case to stick. If we're right and Joan is being framed, she should go free; if not, she needs to pay his bill and accept the jury's decision."

"Agreed."

"Rance needs to be on board, and I need some way of convincing him to let me work with you." I was counting on Paul knowing exactly what Rance would need.

"No NDA," Paul said. "Rance won't expect me to sign one. I can keep my mouth shut, and I promise to keep this between us unless it will affect the case."

"And who decides that?" This was my case, not his.

"Unless it's urgent, you will." He sipped his coffee and watched me.

He was hiding something. Too many vague statements when he could easily give details was a sure tip off. But was it something that I needed to worry about? Or just his normal cop instinct to keep facts close?

"Urgent like...?" I really wanted to make this work. Not sure when or how I went from 'no way am I working with that asshole' to 'please be trustworthy', but it had happened.

"I need to call for backup. I need to pull you out of a dangerous situation. That kind of thing. Anything else I'll have time to warn you."

No time to get the okay, he would just do what he thought was right. It was probably the best I would get from him. "Until Rance gives the okay, I can only stick to the facts. You can't tell David anything. I'll keep him updated if I think he needs to know something."

"Reasonable. I'm on vacation now, so I won't be bumping into him. Why are you convinced it's a frame-up?"

"The file I saw — the one sent from the police — it's thin. I haven't been able to get a copy of the official one. Rance won't let me take a copy of his. Leigh and David gave me some hypotheticals which lead me to believe it's fifty-plus pages short."

"I can get the original." He pulled out his phone and made a note. "Rance must be worried something will be sprung on him at the last minute."

"Rance doesn't seem too concerned. It might be a test."

"Why would he be testing you?"

The way he asked, it sounded like he thought I was crazy. "I don't know. Maybe to see if I notice?"

"I'll call the Crown's office and see what they got from us." He added that to his list. "How far along are you?"

"How will you get this done while you're on vacation?"

"I'll go in during night shift tonight. People won't question me working a bit of OT. And I'll call a friend in the Crown's office. No one will care."

If it was cops, they would be all over unusual activity. Maybe he knew different. It was his worry, not mine.

A group of happy drunks came in and started ordering drinks in loud voices they probably thought were whispers.

"When will you talk to Rance about me?"

"I'll talk to him tomorrow. There is one more thing," I said. "I got a call tonight. This is something you cannot tell David, no matter what."

"Like a test?"

He wasn't stupid. "Yes."

"Go ahead."

It wasn't a pinkie swear to keep a secret, but it would do. "It was a threat. The voice was disguised. They warned me off the case and when I didn't cave, they threatened me."

He handed me his phone. "Write up everything you remember. On your cell or landline?"

I took a screenshot of the call log. "Cell." I sent him the screenshot and typed in the details of the conversation.

He read the note while I finished my drink.

"I'll see about getting a trace. You know it's probably rerouted right? Through a bunch of servers?"

"Yeah. I figure you have better resources for that. And you'll keep it a secret?" It was too late, I'd given him everything. But I wanted to hear him agree.

"David won't get in your way," he said. "But I won't tell him if you think that's best."

—————

15

My phone woke me up at six am. I'm not an early riser, especially after a long night. I picked it up from the bedside table and glared at it like I could convince the text to disappear. I knew I could ignore it until I was ready, but that wasn't in my nature.

It was from Paul, checking what time we should start. Great, now I had to deal with his hours. I answered with a grouchy emoji and *eight o'clock*. I needed time to really wake up and check with Rance about this new development.

By seven thirty I was showered, dressed, and drinking my first coffee. Rance must have started his day early too, because I already had an answer to my email about working with Paul. He said yes. No conditions, nothing but the one-word answer.

I set up my laptop, said goodbye to David as he headed out, and waited for the security buzzer to alert me that I needed to let Paul in. No way was he getting a code.

Our meeting with Vince was at eleven, and we needed to set up the other interviews. I didn't expect Paul to bring the arrest file so fast, or any answers, but this case needed to get some forward motion.

Promptly at eight, the security buzzer went off. I opened the door and checked that it wasn't some weirdo, and then released the gate.

"I brought food," Paul said, placing a paper bag on the kitchen counter. He put his briefcase on the table next to my laptop.

The bag contained a half dozen bagels and a container of cream cheese. I pulled out a poppyseed bagel and reached into the drawer for a sharp knife to split it and a butter knife to spread the topping. "Did David tell you I was easily bribed?" I pushed an empty mug toward him and nodded toward the coffee maker.

"I remember from when you were at the station," he said. "And I like to chew while I think."

"What have you got?" I wasn't ready for small talk.

"The call is untraceable. That's pretty hard for someone without access to a lot of equipment or experience."

I was more disappointed than surprised. "Okay. Well, I've been threatened before. We should just move on with the case." I said it like I wasn't scared shitless. I was. Every time someone told me to back off or else, I wanted to take their advice. But then I wouldn't solve any cases.

"You know how to protect yourself? Not just with bluster."

"That is my favorite weapon. Look, I'm not going to be shoved into a corner to keep me safe. I'll deal with whatever comes."

He looked at me for a moment like he was going to argue. Then he shrugged and spread cream cheese on his bagel without splitting it. I didn't comment, but what a weirdo.

"Okay, so where so we start?"

"The file?"

"I can't get it until later today — maybe. It's been designated confidential to the investigators on the scene. My friend at the Crown's office is checking and will let me know what's there."

"Who are the investigators?" Maybe that was our way in.

"That's the odd thing. I can't get any names and no one I know is assigned."

"Why would that happen?"

"Maybe someone from another station is working it. It's not usual, but I've seen it before."

His answer was too vague for me to be happy, but it was better than nothing, I guess. "Okay. We're interviewing Vince Carmichael and we need to set up with Jackie Tomasino."

"That's all you have?" He fussed with his briefcase, trying to find room on my little table for an iPad and a paper notebook. "Are we going to work here all the time? It's too small to spread out. We can't put up a murder board."

I grinned. Time to see how flexible he was. "This is my office. I don't do boards, usually. We keep everything online so it's accessible all the time."

I didn't mention the other space behind me. That was my living room and personal space, and a sliding panel hid it from sight until we wanted to watch TV or just hang out on rainy days. It did work as a thinking room, and I kept a lot of office supplies and records tucked into concealed cupboards. The patio was our hangout on any day it wasn't raining or below fifteen degrees Celsius.

"Fine. How do you plan to approach Carmichael?" He moved his briefcase to the floor.

"I've been treating him like he's on our side. Joan thinks

he's innocent, but I don't know. Until we get more leads, I can't rule anyone out."

"I pulled his sheet." Paul tapped the iPad and the screen lit up. "Where do I send it?"

I gave him the link to a shared folder on my cloud account. "Anything interesting?"

He sent the PDF and waited for me to open it. There was a list of arrests, most of which Vince didn't get charged on. I couldn't see any useful information, but maybe it was a cop thing. Like he knew why Vince skated so often.

"You have a list of names, right?"

"It's in the folder marked 'leads'."

He opened the file and added some names before closing it again to save his changes and so I could see what he'd done.

"I added the names of a few more cops. The ones on his arrest records."

"It might not be cops," I said. I glanced through the new names. "What about the people I already had?"

"They were part of the arrests too," he said. "This would be easier on a board, but I'll go through and add the connections to your spreadsheet."

"You think we can interview cops without raising suspicion?" I hadn't started to plan that part of the job. Partly because I had no idea who to talk to, but also because I didn't want pissed off cops getting in the way if I could avoid it.

"Not yet, and maybe not in the regular way. I have some contacts that might help with that."

"Who?" I didn't like him keeping secrets. I had no problem with keeping them myself, but it was my case. He worked for me.

"I can't tell you."

I let it go for now. "Do Jackie and Vince know you?"

"I'm Homicide, I don't do other criminal cases."

"So you being a cop won't cause a problem?"

"We don't have to tell either of them," he said.

I called the number I had for Jackie Tomasino, Joan's rival.

"I heard you were on the case, Ms. Deacon," he said, instead of hello. "You want to talk, we do it where I say and when. Agreed?"

I figured it would work better if I let him have his own way, at least at the beginning. "Agreed. Where and when?"

He set us up at his business the next day at seven pm.

16

Vince's wife introduced herself at the front door and pointed us to the side of the house. "He's on the patio watching the grandkids."

I led Paul around to the back, where a boy and a girl chased a puppy around the yard. Vince beckoned us to join him. A carafe and two extra mugs sat on the table in front of him.

"Help yourself," he said.

We sat. Paul took coffee, but I wanted to maintain a business atmosphere to counter the stage setting. Vince might be the grandpa here, but he was the second in command of a criminal organization. If he thought I would ignore that, he was wrong.

We'd agreed that I would lead the questioning, and Paul would come in if he thought I missed something. The goal was to figure out if Vince was guilty of the frame or the murder, and to get more names to investigate. I mean, who should know Joan's enemies better than her right-hand man?

"Cute kids," I said. Let him think he'd fooled me. "You sure you want to talk in front of them?"

"They won't pay any attention to us. New puppy. Just don't start yelling, they'll be fine."

I pulled out my notebook and saw Paul put his phone on the table with the mic end facing Vince.

"You mind if we record this?" I asked.

"Whatever," Vince said. He was doing a good job of pretending there was no problem.

"You know we've been hired to find out who's framing Joan Tiller, right?"

"I know she got her lawyer to hire you. No one said anything about a cop." He picked up his mug and took a sip, keeping his eyes firmly on Paul. "Not sure it's a good idea for me to talk with him here."

If I could send Paul away without looking like I'd handed control to Vince, I just might. But he was here, and Vince was stalling. "He's not a cop right now," I said. "My client is fine with him helping out."

"Joan said it was okay?" He raised an eyebrow, like he'd caught me in a lie.

"Rance is my client. If you don't want to talk with Paul here, I'll let Rance know you won't cooperate. I'm sure Joan will be fine when he passes that on to her."

Paul shifted in his chair. Was he trying to tell me something? I didn't care if he was. He'd agreed to let me run the interview.

"You can't blame me for trying," Vince said. He gave me a grin that was probably charming in his youth; from an old man, it wavered between creepy and pathetic.

"You're wasting time," I said. "Look, I need to be sure you aren't behind this. The murder or the frame."

"You sure she's being framed?"

Paul coughed like he wanted permission to speak.

"You think she killed Kingston?" I asked. "Why?"

"Kingston could be mouthy. Joan likes to be... respected. Even by the guy she shared a bed with."

"Do you have any proof?" If he did, then my case was done. No more Paul interfering — helping — in my case. No more meetings with Joan.

"No," Vince said. He looked over at the kids when one of them shrieked. He didn't go to the rescue, so it was probably a shriek of excitement.

I ignored the noise and made a note to look into Kingston deeper. "If she's being framed, who do you think would do it?"

"You think it's me, right. Power play?" He shook his head and glanced at the grandkids again. "I didn't kill Kingston. I was in Seattle making some business arrangements. Before you ask, no I will not give you details. I didn't order a hit, Kingston wasn't worth the fee."

All fairly easy to check. Maybe Paul could search through the financials for suspicious activity. "And the frame? How do I know you don't want to take over?"

"I make enough money where I am. I'm enough of a target as second. If I took over, I'd have a fight to keep my position. I like being here with the kids. I like knowing my family is fairly safe. Joan's good at her job."

His words rang true to me. The way he kept flicking his eyes to watch behind me, he came across as a family man. I couldn't remove him completely from the list of suspects because this whole meeting was stage managed to give me that impression, but my priority was to get more leads.

"Who might?" I asked.

"Kill Kingston?" Vince asked. "Someone who wanted to get closer to Joan? No one in our organization. They know she'd move on from him soon. Joan doesn't make permanent relationships. Someone Kingston pissed off?"

"Names? I can't get Joan back on the streets without names." I hated to think that was what I was doing, getting her back on the streets. But it was, and as much as I felt better about stopping an injustice, Joan was a criminal and belonged behind bars.

"He had friends. I'll tell them to talk to you. Give me your book and I'll write them out."

I had five new leads to follow, just for the murder. If I could find the actual murderer, then Joan would be freed. It might be easier to do that than find and prove a frame-up. But that was my job: finding out who framed Joan, if that was the reality. "And framing Joan?"

"Jackie Tomasino is the only name I can come up with. Anyone else would just put out a hit. Him and Joan play games. Joan can still run the organization from prison, but it's harder. He'd like making it harder."

Paul leaned forward. "Why not take over the territory?" he asked. I guess he was tired of giving me hints that he wanted to talk.

Vince poured himself more coffee, as if he needed time to think about his answer. "Okay, I get an outsider might look at it like that. Here's the thing about players like Joan and Jackie. Relatively small operations, right? We know who we're fighting with. We all play the game at the same level. One of us gets bigger, then we're competition for the bigger guys. That's sure death."

Vince didn't know about the merger talks. Interesting. "So, if someone wanted to take over Joan's business, it's more likely to be someone ready to play with the big bad wolves," I said. "Or one of them coming at her."

"See, you get it." Vince added cream to his coffee. "You

got any other questions? I want to go back to playing with the puppy."

"Cops," Paul said. "Would one of them try to get rid of her?"

Vince paused with his mug halfway to his lips. I saw his eyes narrow for a split second before he got himself under control. "I'm not giving you names of cops. The ones I know about? They got too good a deal to fuck it up by stirring shit."

17

P aul sent me the recording of the interview; you never knew what you'd find when you listened ten or twenty times to the same answers. We'd debriefed, agreed on our approach with Jackie Tomasino, and he'd left to continue looking for the original case report. I didn't understand why it was hard to find. Even if it was locked down, it should've been on the system, or in a filing drawer. But since I had no way of getting it without him, I let Paul deal with it.

I'd listened to the recording several times and gone through my notes. All I could glean was that Vince had successfully kept the answers short and given us only a few more names. And if he didn't know about Joan and Jackie's plans to merge the businesses, he wouldn't have a motive to stop them. My research had filled the last couple of hours without moving the case forward.

I'd done a social media search on the five names Vince wrote in my book. Desi Ridden, not much activity. Vince noted he was in the same business as Kingston and free-lanced in his spare time. So, fellow muscle but unlikely to advertise that on the various platforms. I'd look on the dark web if he didn't respond to the voicemail I left at his contact number.

Kingston's old flame Inga Sutton didn't look suspicious online, but you never knew. Was she responsible for framing Joan in an attempt to punish her for stealing a lover? Really high risk plan. And real life usually didn't play out like a soap opera. I made a note to reach out to her after our talk with Jackie.

Mike Ball was an old high school friend who, according to his posts, was a criminal, but that was all bluster. A real gang member wouldn't post his badassery on social media. I put him at the bottom of the list. Framing Joan wouldn't help him, and killing Kingston would take away his only contact with that world.

Sherry Waters had no social media presence. Vince noted she was an arms dealer. She'd have no reason to frame Joan, but maybe to kill Kingston? Paul and I would drop in on her rather than set up a meeting. He should be able to find a location if I couldn't get it any other way.

The last name on the list was Joe. No surname, and his contact information was for a martial arts studio. He trained Kingston, and a few others in the same line of business. I struggled to think of a motive for either crime. He might give us a lead or two, though. His studio closed an hour ago, so I planned a drop in tomorrow morning.

That was it. The result of the only productive day so far. Nothing promising, and nothing really off the plate. It was possible Joan did kill Kingston and set up a few clues that she'd been framed to confuse the investigation, but I couldn't think why she would go to the trouble. If she wanted him dead for some reason, the cops would never have found the body.

If there were two crimes here, that might explain why we weren't getting anywhere. A murder and a frame-up by two different people. Someone killed Kingston for a reason unrelated to Joan's gang. And someone jumped on the opportunity to frame Joan and get her out of the way.

Vince had been protective of his pet cops. Maybe because he knew Paul was a cop. Maybe because he used them to get rid of Joan, despite his talk of liking his supporting role. Or the cops killed Kingston and framed Joan, and Vince was scared. I didn't get that vibe off him, but he would be skilled at hiding fear, given the world he inhabited.

I needed to bounce these ideas off someone, and the only person I had was Paul. I reached for my phone to send him a text to meet when a call came in. Blocked number. I almost ignored it, but I didn't.

"You are working with the wrong guy," a woman said, her voice cold. It made me think there was some kind of alteration happening again. Maybe I was talking to a man, or a woman, or an AI.

I wouldn't take too much away from another anonymous threat. "Really? Who should I work with?" If I could make the call last, maybe it would be easier to track this time.

There was a pause, long enough that I wondered if she'd walked away, leaving me to end the call. "You should drop the case, but maybe you're not that smart."

Always a good idea to insult the person you want to cooperate with you.

"It doesn't take brains to know I'm getting close if you're calling." Okay, yes it was a bluff, but something had triggered this call and maybe I just didn't see how close we were to finding the answers.

"Stupid people take risks. You know your partner is dirty, right?"

Paul wasn't my partner, but it wasn't worth clarifying. "You have proof?"

"He's been questioned about money that he shouldn't have. Got charged too."

The only people who would know that were cops, or people cops told. "He's still a detective," I said.

"Yeah. The right friends can cover up anything. You keep working with him and you get all that dirt on you."

The call had gone on long enough. I didn't believe her. David wouldn't have brought Paul to me if he was corrupt. Yes, I'd ask, but like I said, Paul hadn't been fired or put in jail. "You have anything more to say?"

The call ended. I hoped it was because she realized the threat hadn't worked, but I had a sinking feeling that she'd done her job. A tiny seed of doubt was germinating. I knew I didn't trust cops on principle, but I had to believe that most of them were straight. I'd follow up on Paul's background and tell him about the call. See how he reacted.

18

I sat at my dining table and wondered what to do about the call. Last night, I'd tried to reach out to Paul for an explanation, but only got his voicemail. The texts I sent went unread. I needed answers and I wouldn't make David betray a friend to get them. Because Paul was David's friend, and David was the one who brought him to me, I filed the anonymous tip about Paul under 'interesting, but probably a lie or not the whole truth'. I didn't make any notes for someone to read and misunderstand. I didn't just blow it off because people kept secrets from friends, but Paul would get a chance to explain before I told him to step away from the case.

Now, as far as I knew, Paul was off on his mysterious cop/not-a-cop searches of the police records. I was beginning to think that the fact the files were missing should be enough to drop the charges against Joan. I'd asked Rance about it this morning, but he said there were two problems with relying on that. One, if there was a surprise in the records, the opposition would spring it at the worst time. Yes, he'd object, and get time to deal with it, but the damage would be done. And two, even if a judge agreed that the file he had was too thin to prosecute on, Joan would still be under suspicion. She wanted to walk away free and clear.

Rance also didn't seem too worried that I hadn't made progress. He counted on the evidence being hard to find, but when I found it, that would end the case against her. "It will be in a file somewhere or on an interview recording, or someone will slip in a lie. You'll figure it out."

He had way more confidence in me than I did.

Since everyone was so sure it was a frame-up, but had no clue or wouldn't pass on a name of who killed Kingston, I decided to come at it from another angle. Every name on the list I'd gathered so far could be the killer. I listed their names and tried to figure out their motives. Mostly it came down to a power play or a payback scenario; even the five names I got from Vince didn't bring up any novel ideas. I added the word *cop?* to the list because everyone mentioned them, but no one named them. Then I added *cop 2?* because I immediately came up with multiple motives.

I wanted to be better prepared for our interview with Jackie, so I kept thoughts of the threatening call out of mind. I could talk to Paul about the accusation before or after, and whatever he said wouldn't change the fact that we would talk to Jackie.

Okay, so I tried to put it in the recesses of my mind, but I couldn't quite let it go. If Paul was corrupt, then being on the case was the best way to make sure Joan went to prison. I added *cop 3* to the list, mentally adding Paul's name beside it.

My phone rang and I answered it without looking.

"Ms. Deacon," a pleasant female voice asked.

"Yes." Until I knew what she wanted, I would treat her as a potential spam caller or a prospective client.

"I'm calling for Mr. Jackie Tomasino. You have a meeting with him today."

He was trying to get out of the interview. "Yes."

"His plans have changed. Is it possible for you to come now? At the Bayshore Hotel? The tasting room?"

Did he know where I lived? Or was the location just a coincidence? A message? Fuck, I hate this between-the-lines shit. "I can be there in a half hour," I said, in case it was a coincidence. It was a popular hotel and had lots of conferences. Maybe he was at a gang leader symposium.

"That will be acceptable. Thank you for being so flexible."

I said my goodbyes and sat back. My address wasn't public, but I guess I could be traced if someone was truly determined. Or if they had access to police files. I'd made a few statements to the authorities in my career and every single time they'd taken down my full contact details.

19

I dawdled on the walk to the Bayshore because I wanted to reinforce the idea I'd come from some-where else. I'd left Paul a text that the meeting tonight had been rescheduled, but not the new time and place. I didn't want him showing up just as I got into a flow. I still held on to a bit of suspicion, and he wasn't calling me back. The meeting was in a public place, so there wasn't much risk.

A siren burped behind me. I turned to see who was in trouble, and why. A cruiser rolled slowly past then sped up, pulled a U-turn and drove past me again. If I'd brought attention to Jackie, he'd just leave, so I waited until the cruiser disappeared before walking the short distance to the hotel.

Jackie sat alone at a table in the corner, his back to the wall. He was in his mid-sixties, and by the look of his barely thinning hair and lack of wrinkles, he took care of himself. He wore a dark blue suit with a crisp white shirt and no tie.

Three other tables were occupied with men who were suspiciously well-built and wearing jackets roomy enough to hide weapons. The bartender was standing quietly, waiting for someone to need a drink. I was the only woman in the room.

He waved me over and asked if I'd like a glass of wine.

"I'll stick with water," I said. "I'm not much of a day drinker."

He smiled and nodded toward the bartender.

"You know why I want to talk to you," I said, taking my notebook and phone out. "Is it okay if I record? It helps me pay attention to you and not lose anything valuable."

"I'm not confessing to anything," he said. "Go ahead."

I started the recording app and then waited while the bartender placed a tall glass of iced water on a paper coaster, then left.

"I've heard about you, Ms. Deacon. I have reason to owe you a favor."

Did I want criminals owing me favors? Not really, but maybe this meeting would make us even. "Not sure why," I said.

"The work you did to... interfere with the Russian mob activity. It took the pressure off people like me. Old time family organizations."

"Were they trying to take over your territory?"

He glanced at the phone. "I wouldn't say such a thing. But you are here about my friend, Joan. I hear such awful things about what is happening."

"Why do you care?" I asked.

He was charming me despite my better instincts. This man was a criminal, not a harmless businessman worried about his family's future. He did a better job at it than Vince had done with kindly grandfather act, but it *was* an act. I figured he wanted to tell me something. Otherwise he wouldn't be here.

His posture straightened. "We don't like interference. If there is a problem, we are capable of dealing with it within our own system of justice. If someone is framing Joan Tiller, I might be next."

"Who do you think is doing it?"

"I have some suspicions, but they're all obvious. Vince, but he's not ambitious. Someone in her gang, but I don't have names. Other than me, who are you looking at?"

I guess I should feel good that he wasn't dancing around the subject. He was another person who thought the frame was real. I hoped we were all correct about that, otherwise I was spending time getting a murderer free.

"I can't tell you names."

"Afraid I will retaliate against them." He nodded his approval. "Good. I didn't do it. The murder or the frame-up. But Joan has some people Vince won't talk about to you. Some cops on her payroll who were getting pissed at her."

It would be nice to have some names to follow up on, but I'm not sure I'd be ready to believe him. He could be setting me up for something. I still needed the information. "And you know their names?"

"It can't get back to me," he said. "I have my own... relationships to protect. I don't want to find myself in Joan's position. Whoever it is will get better with practice."

His world couldn't survive without corrupt authorities. "It won't."

He glanced over at the closest henchman and nodded. The man stood and walked over with a legal-sized envelope. He placed it on the table in front of me.

Jackie thanked the man and then gestured toward the envelope. "Some proof in there, but the name's Zoe Smith. She's on the take. I don't know exactly what Joan has on her, but she'll be your entry point."

"You think she framed Joan?"

"I'm not sure. I think this will turn out to be more than a single person. But this is the woman I know. Take that home."

The meeting ended and I waited for Jackie and his entourage to leave. I stood in the lobby and saw a white SUV pull around. Jackie and his three companions got in and the vehicle pulled away. As far as I could tell, no one stayed behind to watch me.

———

20

Back at home I started a social media search on Zoe Smith. I didn't expect to get anything proving she was on Joan's team, but getting an idea of her life would give me something to use if we ever decided to interview her.

She seemed like a normal person online. No evidence of the need to be an influencer, or trolling, or some kind of side gig. She posted selfies in pretty locations around town, nothing showing her in uniform. She shared quotes and product sales posts to her friends.

Just goes to prove that you can't trust people until you know them in real life. Maybe not even then. I changed *cop 1* to *Zoe*, and started adding ideas around her name.

Paul replied to a text to say he was coming over, and did I want a latte. Confronting him about the allegations from my mystery caller would go better over a coffee, so I said yes. I cleared up the counter and table to make him more comfortable, because he was obviously not used to cramped quarters and messes.

He arrived within twenty minutes, and I buzzed him

through the security door before stepping outside to watch him walk down the finger dock. The couple of hours I'd spent researching at my laptop left me with a stale feeling. A lungful of fresh-ish air revived me. The sun was shining on the windows of the buildings that stood like sentinels across the road, making it hard to keep my focus in the direction of the street. The usual clinks and ruffles from the sailboats around me were calming.

"I got cookies," Paul said. He held up a bag with the name of my favorite local bakery on the side. In the other hand, he held a cardboard tray with two coffees.

"Good man." I held the door open for him and followed him through.

He tore the bag, exposing a half dozen thumbprint cookies, put the coffees on the table, and looked around for a place to put the tray. I nodded to the counter and then sat and waited for him to settle. I wanted his report before I pressed him on the corruption accusation.

"I checked Vince's alibi," he said. "It held up. And our meeting with Jackie isn't going to happen. He was picked up on racketeering charges an hour ago."

If Jackie thought I had something to do with that, I was in trouble. "He rearranged the interview. I tried to contact you, but I met him three hours ago."

"And?"

I shook my head. "What instigated the arrest?"

"He's been under observation for months. Today he made the mistake of talking to the wrong person in the wrong place — not you. We recorded everything. Pretty solid case, he'll do time."

"Any chance he'll think I had something to do with it?" I was stalling because suddenly I didn't know how to ask him about his past.

"No. Undercover operation. What did he tell you?"

"What about the Tiller file?"

"It wasn't in the documents room, and I don't have the authority to access the computer records."

The main thing I needed from him, and he couldn't deliver. "So does that mean you won't be able to get it?"

"No, don't worry. I've got someone higher up looking into it. My buddy in the Crown office hasn't seen their file, but I should hear tomorrow."

"Okay. Let's hope we get it and there's something in the documents that helps." *And that it doesn't point to you.* I lifted the lid of my laptop to show him my analysis of the potential suspects. "Jackie gave me a cop's name. I guess it's easier to rat out the competition than give up someone on your own books." I pointed to the screen, where Zoe's name was highlighted. "I've been trying to figure out motive and opportunity."

"Don't know the name. I'll check out her record when I get back to the station."

I got that feeling again that there was something weird about him going into the office and digging for information while he was supposed to be on leave. "I got another call."

He jerked upright. "Same person?"

"Female voice, but kind of emotionless, like it was an AI. I kept her on the line as long as possible. I've put the notes in our shared file."

"Did you record it?" He pulled out his phone and started typing.

"No. I don't automatically record and didn't have time to turn it on."

"What did they say?" He was looking at his screen — reading my notes, probably. "Anything that might give us a clue? You know if we can find out who's threatening you, it will give us the answer."

I did know that. There was no reason for anyone to threaten me other than to stop me getting closer to solving the case. I was lucky they stuck with calls for now. I took a bite of a cookie to stall a little longer. But it was time to ask the hard question. "They said you were charged with corruption."

21

"Not charged," he said quietly. "And it's not common knowledge."

"So that might be a clue to the caller's identity?"

"Maybe," he said. "I'm not a corrupt cop, Charity."

"That's all good to say, Paul, but I need more if you expect me to believe you." Every crooked cop or guilty suspect proclaimed their innocence until they were faced with the proof. Or they could prove the truth to their accusers.

"You believe an anonymous caller over me? You've worked with me, Charity."

I nodded because I didn't want to distract him with a conversation about our last cases, and to show I was open-minded. I couldn't believe he could hide criminal activity from David or the other detectives, so I didn't press.

"Okay, yes, I was accused. Professional Standards investigated. I proved I was innocent. How much more do you want to know?"

I understood why this was hard to explain. Just because

he proved his innocence didn't mean suspicion went away. The old where-there's-smoke rule.

"Paul, I want to trust you, but the more you hide the less I can do so. What was the accusation? Who reported you? What was the proof? The details might help with this case."

He stood and paced the tiny area. It wasn't big enough to give him peace only to crank up his... what? Anger, frustration, shame?

He stopped moving and joined me at the table. "I don't like talking about it, but I guess I understand why you can't just take my word without more details. It was a long time ago. When I first told my boss I wanted into Homicide."

"How long ago?" He wasn't that much older than me, or at least he didn't look it.

"Ten years. I've never even taken a free coffee, Charity. Not because I'm some kind of rule follower, but because I know that's how it starts. You take a coffee from someone, then the next thing you get offered is a little more value and comes with a little tiny favor. And within no time, you're on someone's payroll and wondering how to get out alive."

I held off commenting. He was unrolling the story in his head as he spoke. So I'd let him go on as long as he wanted. Not like we had anyone to interview until I got calls back from Kingston's friends.

"The accusation was of taking a bribe to turn a blind eye to a fence's operation. I was working robbery at the time, so it was plausible. Professional Standards looks into every accusation regardless of the likelihood it's true. Nothing is anonymous, but it's all confidential. We aren't supposed to know who accused us."

Probably worried about retaliation. The cops must be like any community; petty jealousies and unfounded rumors would circulate. Professional Standards would be busy all the time if just anyone could throw out accusations. Add to that every criminal and sensitive civilian tossing out lies to get some kind of deal or special treatment, and it would be a nightmare.

"I didn't have that much trouble proving the accusation wasn't true. The person who complained was sloppy. I was out of town on the day I was supposed to be receiving an envelope of cash. It sticks though, the stink of corruption. For a couple of years, I would hear whispering that I was lucky they couldn't prove I took the bribe, but I must be in someone's pocket. It faded away when I got into Homicide and started catching murderers."

And now someone was bringing the whispers back. "Did you ever find out who made the accusation?"

"A cop called Evelyn Moore. I wasn't supposed to know, and I can't remember exactly how I found out. But she's stuck in uniform as a sergeant, desk not streets. I guess wasting Professional Standards time is as bad for your career as being dirty is."

Her name was familiar. "Has she tried anything else?" I asked as I opened my laptop.

"Not to my knowledge. Keeps a low profile. Works in records." He moved to stand behind me as I scrolled through the few documents from the case file.

"She signed most of the arrest records in Joan's file." I wanted to add her to my list of suspects. It was thin, but if she was stuck in her career, was she also working a side gig?

"Not unusual," he said. "Well, not strictly normal either. She would sign as part of her job. But it's weird that she's signed so many. It would mean Joan kept being arrested on her shift. These files cover a couple of years, so not possible."

"Okay, let me add her to our list. Sit down, I can't type

while you watch me." He took his chair again. I put her name where I'd entered *cop 3*. "We have some things to follow up on. Maybe talk to this Zoe Smith or drop in on a few of Kingston's friends."

"Or we could trace this caller." Paul nodded toward my phone as if the threats were the only calls I got. "If someone is taking the time to frighten you off the case, then they are definitely involved."

If I agreed, we'd never get to the interviews, or I'd be doing them alone. I didn't mind so much with Kingston's friends, but interviewing a cop was better done with Paul at my side. "What makes you think you'll be more successful this time?"

"We won't know until we try. You need to turn on the call recording app. Just delete anything personal."

"Is it legal? I thought both of you had to know you were being recorded, and get permission," I said. On my usual cases, it didn't matter; we weren't going to court.

"It's single consent here, but only if you are a participant. You can't record two other people on a call and use it as evidence."

I picked up my phone and found the setting. I activated it and then took a screenshot of the call details just in case. "Done. But we need to move on to the interviews first. I can't have you haring off to what's probably a dead end. We're supposed to be a team, right?"

He looked at me for a long moment. He was hiding something, but maybe it was just frustration at hitting a dead end. "Okay, fair point."

22

He gave up too quickly for me to believe the subject was closed permanently, but moving on was my goal, so I let it go.

"Any of the friends look good for the murder?" he asked.

"No, and that worries me. It's harder to say if they look good for the frame-up, but we need to talk to them. We have time today to go see this martial arts guy in his studio. But Zoe is a better lead."

"She is, but we can't just drag a cop to an interview. She'll call for her union rep at the very least. We need a plan."

He thought we needed to plan for every interview, even if it was as little as agreeing who would lead it. I missed just jumping in and finding out whatever I could, at least on the first try. "How long do we have to wait?"

"I'll bring her here on some pretense." He looked around the space as if he'd forgotten how small it was. "Nothing too threatening. Maybe we say we're trying to help her. Pretend we know everything."

"Why here? I don't like bringing suspects into my

home." I felt stronger about it than dislike, but Paul must have a reason. It's not like I had a place to restrain her.

"Gets her off guard. This place is neutral. She's not under arrest."

"And if she won't talk?"

"I'll threaten to make a complaint," he said. "I'm hoping it won't come to that. We'll need more proof than Jackie's word."

And he knew the consequences of an unsupported accusation, for Zoe and him. "How are you going to get her to come here?"

"I'll give it some thought. Maybe I'll say there's some kind of evidence that came up in the investigation. If she thinks she can stop us from following the lead, she'll come."

"You'll lead the questioning," I said. "I won't get in the way."

"Yes. Look, it's going to take me some time to set this up. I could still get a buddy to follow up on the call. I don't like the idea of us ignoring threats."

I knew the subject wasn't closed. "I'll send you the screenshot I took of the call log again. But this is low priority, Paul. We need the original files, and we need to talk to Zoe. We need to talk to all the names on our list."

He pulled out his phone and checked the text I sent. "This will help."

"I mean it. We need to make progress on this. If Joan is innocent, she shouldn't be stuck in a holding cell. And the real killer needs to be caught."

"I heard you, Charity. Look, I know I've had a hard time getting the file for you. I am trying. How about we set up Zoe for tomorrow morning? I'll send you the time when I get her to agree. Then we can go from her to the list of friends. And we might get a few names from her."

"I need to talk to the people who signed the documentation, too."

He put his phone away and grabbed a cookie. "That should wait until we have the whole file."

Suddenly I felt like I was in a box fighting to get out and do my job. "Why, are you protecting your buddies?"

He grinned and finished chewing the cookie. "I'm not. You start interviewing cops who are just doing their jobs, the blue line will form up and we'll have no chance to talk to anyone. We get our shit together by prioritizing the interviews. Hit what looks like the low-hanging fruit first. You accidentally talk to whoever is in control before we're ready, and we're done. Turn some lackeys and the boss will be in our trap."

I told myself he wasn't being patronizing on purpose. He knew the best way to do the job, and I didn't. Telling my anger to piss off wouldn't work, so I needed to stop feeding it. I kept myself from responding until I could do it without calling him on his tone. It seemed to take forever, but Paul didn't notice.

I finally said, "I guess that's right. I'm not going to sit here waiting for you to show up with Zoe. I'll go see this Joe guy in his martial arts studio while you are out placating egos."

Another grin. "You make it sound so easy. I'll be getting a highly restricted file for you and trying to find out who's threatening you so maybe I can put a stop to it."

23

I headed out to talk to Joe at the martial arts studio. He was the only one of Kingston's friends I'd been able to track down. None of the others responded to any contact through social media, texts, or voicemails.

The studio was in New Westminster, on Sixth Street. An area that saw a wave of development in the eighties. The buildings weren't exactly run down, but they were showing their age. A few new mixed retail and residential buildings highlighted the age of their neighbors. Joe worked out of a second-floor space under the business name First Kick Best Kick.

I found him leading a class of eight-year-olds through a sequence of attacks and blocks. Moms and dads sat in chairs around the edge of the large mats. A few of the parents were watching their children, but most of the moms and a couple of the dads were focused on Joe. I couldn't blame them; he was built in that compact way that didn't scream steroids and weights. He was good-looking too, in a hard man kind of way.

I didn't interrupt the lesson, figuring it would be better

to chat with him without a bunch of witnesses and a small army of pointy elbows and poky fingers.

The kids were good and moved almost like a choreographed troupe. None of them seemed to need to check their position in the mirrors that lined the back wall.

The lesson lasted another ten minutes, and when Joe dismissed the kids with a bow, they turned back into normal loud, excited, and fun children.

"Are you looking for self-defense classes?" Joe was standing beside me. His voice was soft now that he wasn't barking commands.

"Joe?" I asked to make sure it wasn't just some instructor.

"Yeah, this is my dojo. We have classes for women in an hour."

"I'm a private investigator. I have a few questions about Kingston."

Gone was the businessman looking to sell me classes. It was like a shutter rolled up over his eyes. His body tensed, but not like he was going to attack — more defensive than aggressive. "He's dead. They arrested his killer."

"That might not be the case," I said. "I've been retained to make sure the case has no holes." He didn't need to know which side hired me.

"How can it have holes if they arrested her?"

This was not going the way I wanted.

"Let's start again," I said. "My name is Charity Deacon. I've been hired to make sure Joan Tiller wasn't framed. We want to make sure nothing will come up in the court case."

He relaxed a little, keeping his eyes on my face like he was looking for proof I was lying. "Joe Turner. I knew Kingston when we were in school. Not sure I know anything that will help you."

I'd put a lot of money on a bet that he was hiding something. Maybe just a juvenile record, or maybe a little side action now. I wasn't sure how a dojo would work in a money laundering scheme. Of course, he could be working for someone as muscle, too.

"Anything you know will help. To be honest, there aren't a lot of people for me to talk to. He seemed pretty much a loner."

Joe glanced over my shoulder as if someone had walked into the room. I didn't need to turn to see that no one had; the mirror on the wall across from me displayed a full view of the entrance.

"Anything you tell me will be confidential," I said.

"I said I don't have anything," Joe snapped. "I haven't seen him for months. We didn't talk about his work. I didn't want to know who he'd beaten up for that woman."

"Why did Kingston go into that business?" I wasn't planning on giving up until he told me something, or I figured out why he was so determined to distance himself from the dead man.

"Same way most people do, I guess. He was good with his fists. He didn't carry any guilt over a beating. He didn't have any other skills."

"There were other options," I said. "Bouncer, bodyguard."

Joe rolled his eyes at me as if I was incredibly naive. "Bouncer is the way he got hired by the gang. Bodyguards need more than just muscle. They need to carry weapons, and Kingston made some mistakes that kept him from getting a license."

"Mistakes that could have gotten him killed?"

"Long time ago." Joe picked up a towel from the floor and wiped his face. "I need to get ready for the next class."

"Do you know his other friends? Desi, Inga, Mike, Sherry?"

"Yeah, we all went to Templeton. Desi works in the same job as Kingston. Inga works for Joan Tiller. Mike is a gangster wannabe. Kingston kept him out of the life. Sherry... Yeah, she might be pissed off with him for some reason. I can't tell you anything else."

So, all Kingston's friends were from his school days, and two of them worked with Joan's gang. Vince could have mentioned that. "What does Sherry do? I couldn't find her anywhere."

"She works in supply. For the gangs. That's all I got. Now get out."

He knew exactly what Sherry supplied. That could be what he was afraid of telling me. "Thanks, that will help me."

I headed back out onto the mostly empty street. Sherry was my best bet to go to next. I just needed a way to find her. She supplied a gang like Joan's, so drugs? Guns? I called and left Vince a message telling him I'd learned about the connection with the names he gave me and his gang and told him to call me back. He was my best shot at meeting Sherry.

My car was a block away and I was hungry. There were a couple of interesting restaurants in the next block up the hill. East African, Mexican, and Eastern European. My phone pinged with a text before I decided what I wanted to try. Val.

Get in here. I have something you need to see.

Where here?

My work.

Be there in an hour.

She responded with a clock emoji, which I took to mean

hurry up. I gave up on dinner, grabbed a power bar from the convenience store across the street and headed to my car. On the way I called Paul and updated him about the interview.

"I can see if the Waters woman has any previous history," he said.

"Do it. I'm on my way to see something Val found for me."

"Where? I can join you."

"Do you have the file?"

"Not yet. Tomorrow probably, after Zoe's interview."

"Do you have anything new we can use?"

"Not until we've talked to Zoe."

"I'll be fine alone with Val, and I'll let you know what she found." I ended the call before he could try harder to convince me he should join us.

24

I dropped off my car at the usual place and walked the twenty minutes to Rance's office. Maybe it was paranoia, but I saw more than the usual number of patrol cars on the way. No one did anything but drive by, so I didn't make a note of any car numbers.

Val was waiting for me in the lobby of the building and escorted me to Rance's office. She told me to keep quiet until we were in the administration room. We didn't pass anyone on the way, but I did as she asked.

The empty offices were creepy, like every other building I'd been in after hours. All the normal activity of talking, working, breathing haunted the silence. I guess you get used to it if you work late often enough. Val didn't seem to notice anything off about the place.

"I found something while I was digitizing a file that might help. You can't tell anyone I showed it to you," she said when we were sitting at a long table in the back room. A pair of what looked like scanners occupied the far end, and the rest was clear — probably where she sorted and checked the documents. Around us were shelving units filled with banker boxes. I could hear the sound of computer fans whirring from somewhere in the back.

"Is it going to get you fired? You need to be careful." I wasn't going to put her future on the line for a case. If Rance was keeping things from me, there must be a reason.

"I'm not an employee, so he can't fire me," she said, with all the bravado of a twenty-year-old. "Wait here."

She disappeared between two of the shelving racks, returning in a moment with a leather-covered journal.

"I scanned this today, and I mostly don't read the documents — they're pretty boring usually, and I don't have the time. I noticed Joan Tiller's name on a bunch of pages, so I thought it might help you. You can't take it away. It's going to a shredding company when I'm done here, and the auditors check I didn't screw up, so someone might be expecting to see it on a checklist."

She put the journal on the table in front of me, but I didn't open it. "Why do you think Rance didn't show it to me? I'm not looking until I'm sure you won't get in real trouble, Val."

"I won't. Don't worry about me. I always take care of myself."

Val hadn't relied on anyone since the time when her sister brought her to work the streets. I know they didn't have a lot of options, but then after we rescued her, Emma had just disappeared on Val.

"Then why did I have to keep quiet as we walked through an empty office?"

She rolled her eyes at me and then sighed. Still acting like the teenager I first met. "Fine. There's a couple of paralegals here that want my ass out of the office. I think one of them is still here. No big deal; if Rance ends my contract, then I'll find other clients. Just like you do."

"And how will that affect your relationship with Rory? You live in Rance's pool house, with his son."

"We can find another place. If Rory takes his dad's side, then he's not the right guy for me. And Rance is cool."

Her face tightened as she casually dismissed the relationship with Rory. She put on a hard attitude, but they were perfect for each other. And Rory knew her history and didn't care.

"You didn't answer my question. Why wouldn't Rance show me this?"

She glanced down at the journal. "I don't know. It wasn't in the right box, but lots of stuff gets misfiled. It's in his handwriting, so maybe he thought he'd transcribed the contents. It's about her, his thoughts and some details about her previous arrests. He's been her lawyer for years."

It could be innocent, but given the lack of documentation and the so-far useless leads, I wasn't ready to dismiss it as an innocent mistake. I flipped open the cover and started reading. Rance had beautiful penmanship, but his notes were just a word or two here and there. Something to remind him of the full content, was my guess.

"It's going to take a while," I said. "Can I just take photos of the pages?"

"Yeah. I can't print you a copy because there are records, but no one will know you used your phone."

I scanned every page before I used the camera. There were twenty-five related to Joan. The rest were about other local criminals. I knew Rance was a criminal lawyer, but it looked like he was doing a lot of work for Joan's people. I took photos of all the pages, whether Joan was mentioned of not. If Rance was working for Joan for more than legal advice and services, maybe there was something pointing to his being a mob lawyer. I hoped not, but I couldn't ignore the voice inside that was screaming there was something wrong in this case.

"He's got a lot of notes about the cops involved in her past arrests," I said. Was it confirmation that there were crooked cops involved? I saw Evelyn Moore's name mentioned more than once. "I recognize some of the names. This is going to help, thanks."

What I didn't see was any connection to our elusive Sherry Waters. Although, he'd interviewed Zoe Smith twice for an alibi. Interesting.

"Why is this one so hard?" Val asked. "I mean, you usually solve cases really fast."

"Someone is blocking us," I said. "I don't know who exactly, but I'm going to find them. If Joan didn't kill the guy, then someone else did, and maybe just to get her arrested."

"You finished with the book?"

"Yeah. Make sure you put it back in the same box," I said. "In case someone here purposely misfiled it. I don't want them to know anyone found it."

"Any way you can make it so the two paralegals are involved? I'm here for probably another six months, so it would be great to remove my least favorite assholes."

"You have favorite ones?"

"Don't laugh. I do, but they're just corporate ones who don't pick on me."

"I'll ask you the same question you asked me: why is this job taking so long?" I asked to avoid getting into the bitch session on rules and regulations that came with every big business job. Val was like me in that she thrived in a more flexible environment. We were people the rule followers might call cowboys, at best.

"There's years of paper to put through the scanners, and the current stuff gets done too. I have help, but we have to index everything, so we get through maybe a box a day of the old stuff, sometimes even less. When we're done, I'll have the process written out so they can hire people to keep it going. It's kind of nice to have a regular income, but I can't wait to work on something more interesting."

25

I waited for Paul to make it down the finger dock to my door. He was alone. I expected him to bring our suspect, Zoe Smith, the corrupt cop. But no. It seemed like I would never get my way with this guy. Was it because he still didn't think I should be involved in police matters? Or were my expectations too high? If our positions were reversed, and I'd made a change in plans, what would I have done? I liked to think the answer was call him and keep him up to date, but I guess if I was honest that wasn't true. Although come to think of it, I'd been good at reaching out to him, just not patient if we didn't connect.

It was possible the problem was all in my paranoia. Just because she wasn't walking ahead of him, being subtly herded toward her fate, didn't mean anything big had gone wrong.

"Don't panic, she's on her way," he said when he reached my door. "Pretending she was coming to talk to a suspect guarantees she'll show."

A good plan, actually.

"When?" I asked.

"About five minutes from now." He handed me his briefcase and tipped his head to my door. "Go inside. I'll wait at the security gate like I'm keeping an eye on you. We can talk about what else I brought after."

I didn't argue. Just because he was ordering me around didn't mean he was in charge. I had five minutes to look inside his case. "It will look more real if you wait outside." I gave him my security code.

He smiled at me and turned to walk back to the street.

Inside, I double checked that the area was free of anything Zoe could use as a weapon. Yes, she'd have her sidearm, but Paul would take care of that. I'd hate to explain how our main lead got away by bashing us over the head with a frying pan.

Since I'd gone through this three times already in the last hour, there was nothing to clear away. I put Paul's case on the counter and flipped the clasps. He hadn't bothered to lock it, or had unlocked it before coming in. There was one file inside, a big fat one, maybe sixty or more pages thick. The case file.

I heard voices outside my door just before a knock. Still keeping the pretense up that I was the suspect, I closed the case and put it on the kitchen floor where Zoe wouldn't see it.

I opened the door. Paul introduced both of them and asked to come inside.

"Why?" I asked, getting into the role.

"We have some questions."

"Do I need a lawyer?"

Paul gave me a look that said I should stop playing and let them in. "No. Just a few questions."

I stood aside and closed the door behind Zoe, flipping the deadbolt quietly.

"Have a seat," I said, pointing to the three chairs I'd placed strategically around the table. Zoe did as I hoped and took the farthest, so she faced the door. Now she had no easy escape with me and Paul between her and the exit, but thought she was being smart about her choice.

She was petite. I know there were no height requirements for being a cop, but I always expected one to be big and intimidating. I guess the uniform and training brought on the intimidation.

I nodded to Paul to start talking. We'd agreed he'd start the questions because she was more likely to answer him than me at first.

"Zoe, I'm sorry, but we aren't here to question Charity."

"What the fuck?" Her voice was raspy and had an edge of anger beyond the words.

"We've been given a tip about you," he said. "Someone is claiming you're on Joan Tiller's payroll."

A bit aggressive, but how else were we going to get to the point?

"Who?"

"Are you denying it?" he asked.

"I'm asking who told you," she said. "Someone you believe, I see. What happened to the blue line?"

Paul waited. A good technique to use with a suspect, but Zoe had the same training.

It felt like forever before she started talking. "I want my lawyer present. And we're not doing this here. Why are we here and not at the station, anyway? Where are Professional Standards?"

Time for me to take over. "We want to hear your side of it before formal complaints get lodged. You know how that can affect your career."

She huffed and crossed her arms protectively across her

chest. "Oh, you're both trying to protect me? Give me a break."

"If you're innocent, yes," I said. "The stink of an accusation never goes away. Tell us what happened."

She ignored me and kept looking at Paul. "You working with Professional Standards now? This isn't protocol. If you have a valid complaint, press the charge. I'll get to face the accuser that way, give them something to regret."

The bravado wasn't sitting right. Her body language was all about protection. Her arms were crossed. Her posture was like she was ready to leap the table and escape. Her face flushed and then went pale.

"Just come clean," Paul said.

She stood and leaned in to shout in his face. "Why? You'll believe me? I'll feel better? This is bullshit. I'm leaving."

She moved to walk around me to the door and realized her path was blocked. A benefit of a small home, I guess.

"Get out of my way." She shoved me hard enough to rock the chair. "You can't keep me here."

If we didn't do something, we'd be stuck in her denials until she called for backup. Paul just sat back in his chair as if this was the most normal way to interrogate a colleague.

"Look, you can do what you choose," I said. "If you leave here without talking to us, then you'll face charges. If you stay and tell us what happened to put you in this position, we can try to get you help. If you haven't gone too far over the line, then I'm sure a deal can be made."

I wasn't confident, but maybe Paul knew a way. If she was the one who killed Kingston and framed Joan, she was lost. I did believe Jackie's tip. There was guilt there in all her protestations. But a killer? I wasn't so sure.

26

Zoe just sat there, arms crossed, looking down at the tabletop. I was sure she wasn't checking out the wood grain. If I was in her position, I'd be making a mental list of pros and cons and wondering how long I could bluff and what would happen if I couldn't convince Paul that I was innocent. She wouldn't be worried about me. I had no official standing.

We needed her to break, and I needed it to be fast. That file was calling to me. I forced myself not to peek in the direction of the briefcase. Or to look at him to speed things along. Zoe would talk easier if we left the decision to her.

She looked up at us and I saw defeat on her face. Her mouth turned down and was firmly shut. Did that mean she'd decided to let Professional Standards take over? Not helpful to my reputation if the cops told Rance that Joan was off the hook before I could, but if Zoe confessed to the murder, my case would close. I'd get paid and I could move on to easier jobs. Ones that didn't include working with cops.

"May I have a glass of water?" she asked.

Paul stood and took the two steps to my kitchen. He opened every cupboard until he found the disposable cups — no glass to make into a weapon. A control tactic. If he wanted to do it fast, he would have asked me which cupboard to go to.

He placed the cup in front of her and sat again. I waited while she swallowed half the contents in one gulp.

"I made a mistake," she said, putting the cup on the table. "I needed cash fast."

"So you borrowed from Joan?" I asked.

She huffed and rolled her eyes. "I'm not that stupid. I got a tip on a horse. I bet a little, just testing the reliability of the tip, right?"

"It was a hustle," Paul said. "You won, right?"

"Yeah. Not enough for what I needed, but I could see the end to my problems if I bet bigger and won."

"So you made another bet?" I'd think her smarter if she'd just borrowed the cash.

"Three. I just rolled the winnings to start, and on the third, I put in everything I had plus money I borrowed from my mother's account." She shrugged like it was nothing. "I lost. I was in a worse hole than when I started. Then the phone rang. Joan."

Putting Joan in prison for murder wouldn't solve Zoe's problem. The debt would stay with the gang.

"She said she'd help me out. I'd get the full amount I would have won, so I could pay back the account and I'd have the money I needed. Just had to do a few favors. Nothing too big."

"What did you need the money for?" Paul asked. I thought he was interrupting the flow of information.

"I don't want to say. It all seemed smart at the time, but now? I was stupid."

"How much?" I asked. Paul wasn't the only one who wanted to look like he was in control.

"At the end? Fifty grand. It started out as ten grand. It added up really fast." She rubbed her eyes with her fingers.

"So, what favors?" I asked.

"Mostly a heads up if an investigation got too close. Or I heard someone was making a deal with the Crown. Nothing like murder. I know now it's all the same, really, but then? I thought it was nothing."

"How long have you been doing it?" I asked. Part of me sympathized. Getting in this kind of mess didn't require an active decision to go bad. Just a series of stupid mistakes.

"Two years. I was almost out of it," Zoe said. "Joan told me I only had to do one more favor and I would be finished."

Maybe she'd been telling the truth, but I didn't trust Joan to keep her promise. "What was the one thing?" I asked.

"Find out who killed Kingston. I had no idea how to do it, but I was trying." She turned to me. "She told me to keep you in the dark."

So, Joan had more people on the case than just me. I wondered how Rance would feel about that. I knew I didn't like it for two reasons: it was my job to complete, and if anyone got in the way, I would fail.

"How were you trying?" Paul asked. "Did you get a lead?"

"I had some suspicions about other cops," she said. "It's not like we hang out in a club for corrupt officers, but you notice shit when you're on someone's payroll. You see other cops acting like they have a secret."

"Let's say we believe you," Paul said. "Who should we look at?"

"I'm not a snitch," she said, with all the self-right-eousness of a crook pretending to be legit.

"You want a chance to save your career?" Paul asked. "Then you tell us what you know."

"Let me turn myself in," she said. "If you don't drag me into the station, I get to sort out my stuff and tell people I care about what happened."

"Tell us who you think is in the gang and tell me why you needed the money that started the whole thing." He was going to let her leave, and I didn't argue. She didn't kill Kingston or frame Joan. She was just a stupid kid who was facing consequences.

"I needed the money because my boyfriend was going into rehab. I was so happy he was ready, but I needed to pay for a good place."

"Did he get help?" I asked. If he had, at least some good had come from her actions.

"No. He OD'd while I was placing bets."

"I'm sorry," I said. "Just tell us the rest."

"There's definitely some kind of organized corruption," she said. "I wasn't close enough to find names, but Joan told me a few stories that made it obvious."

So, nothing more than what we had; guesses but no leads.

"Did you keep records of your investigation?" Paul asked.

"On my phone." She pulled it out and tapped the screen a couple of times. "I can send it to you."

Paul gave her an email address and checked to make sure he'd received the document. "Okay. We'll take it from here. You have until end of shift, or I'll call Professional Standards."

I had no idea when end of shift was, but it meant some-thing to Zoe.

"I only need a couple of hours. Do you think I'll be able to keep my job?"

Paul shrugged. "It will depend on everything you told Joan. If you're lucky, you'll be in uniform for the rest of your days on the force, and every time someone suspects you did another favor, they'll pull you in for an interview."

She thanked him again and left, unlocking the door like she owned the place.

27

"I'm starving," Paul said. "Can we go out somewhere and eat?"

"I want to go through that file you brought," I said. I was hungry too, but I'd waited too long for proof that Rance's file was missing vital information. "And what she just sent you."

"You looked in my briefcase?"

"You left it unlocked."

"I know. We'll look at it over dinner," he said. "Your place is too small to spread out the papers and have food."

I couldn't deny the truth of that, but sitting at a table in a busy restaurant didn't quite seem the right way to go either. It wasn't prime dinner time, but we wouldn't have any place to ourselves.

"Can we just have a peek first?" If I got an idea of the volume of data in the file, I could eat first.

"Nope, I know a place we can go and still have privacy. You like Chinese food, right?"

I nodded. "You mean the Pearl Garden?" The dining room was lined with quiet booth-like spaces. Not exactly rooms, but we wouldn't be overheard if we talked quietly. And it was only a half hour walk so we wouldn't have to drive. I didn't plan on having to take Paul somewhere or be driven home, if we argued about the next steps.

He grabbed his bag, and we headed up the finger dock to the street.

The street lights were on, but Vancouver never got that dark with the headlights and the various store fronts blazing until the wee hours.

The restaurant was in Chinatown, which was only a block or two past Gastown. We went down Cordova Street, avoiding the hustle on Hastings. The sidewalk was closed about three blocks before our destination. A big hole in the gutter needed repair, but no one was working this late. I didn't like the look of the narrow covered walkway against the building.

"The other side is clear," I said, pulling Paul after me to cross in the short traffic break.

A siren burped just as we reached the other side of the street. A cruiser pulled over toward us. I hadn't noticed them. But then, I wasn't looking for anything but a clear path.

"Jaywalking? Give me a break." I waited for the cruiser to stop, prepared for a lecture or a ticket. I didn't care — whatever got us on our way the fastest.

Paul stepped in front of me and flashed his badge. The driver moved on with a nod. I wasn't completely sure, but I thought he looked like one of the cops who hassled me in the station.

"Let's go," Paul said.

I told him my suspicions.

"I'll check who is supposed to be using the cruiser. I'm

more concerned that I used my badge. It was just automatic. Now they know I'm with you."

So, he wasn't used to subterfuge — or 'undercover' as he would call it. It made me a bit more comfortable about our agreement. The fact that he was sure it was cops running the frame bothered me. I mean, *I* thought it was, but like Zoe said, shouldn't he be holding the blue line?

I was too hungry to question him now, and too interested in the contents of the file.

28

We got a booth in the far corner of the restaurant, with no other diners around and far enough from the kitchen that we wouldn't have a stream of servers passing by.

"You want anything in particular?" Paul asked.

"I'm flexible. Probably won't eat the eyes if we have fish, but that's all."

He placed the order in Cantonese and the waiter left.

"You're full of surprises." I didn't know anything about his background, which made me feel a bit like an asshole. I'd worked with him for long enough that I should know he spoke different languages. In fact, I should know he liked Chinese food, and whether or not he had kids, or a wife.

"Grew up in Hong Kong. Before the handover."

Well, he wasn't all that forthcoming even when I asked, so maybe I shouldn't feel bad.

"Why did you agree to let Zoe turn herself in?" I wasn't willing to sit in silence until the food came, and I didn't want to be interrupted in the middle of reviewing the file. This was the best I could come up with.

He unrolled the chopsticks from his napkin and studied them as he spoke. "She might run," he said. "She can't go far in the time I gave her. Her financials didn't show any source of money if she fled, and she has family here."

"If she isn't the person who framed Joan or killed Kingston, I guess I shouldn't care." My stomach growled as I caught the scent of frying onions and garlic.

"But you do," he said. "You don't like letting go if you can't control the play."

I also didn't like him assessing me and sharing his opinion, no matter how accurate he was. "Maybe."

The server put bowls in front of us, giving me a fork even though I hadn't asked for one. In moments, there were five dishes steaming on the turntable. I recognized a couple — sort of — like the vegetable chow mien. Others I'd never seen before, like the thin strips of brown meat, or perhaps mushroom.

The server checked with Paul and then left.

"Dig in," he said. "We'll clear some space when we've had some food."

I tried everything, and in about ten minutes my hunger was sated. I stared at the file like it was dessert.

Paul put both our empty bowls on the turntable and opened the file between us.

"It's way more detail than Rance showed me," I said. "Can I give this to him when we're done?"

"No. I have to get it back right away. I'll get a copy sent over. If you pass it on, he'll have too many questions."

"Send me the info from Zoe," I said, and then remembering the book I'd reviewed with Val, I added, "I can send you a bunch of pictures of Rance's notes."

"Does he know you have them?" He sent me the file from Zoe.

"No."

"Then just summarize and log it in the spreadsheet. I can't read his notes without express permission. If it leads to an arrest, I could end up screwing the case."

Fair enough. I sent myself a reminder. "What about Zoe's info?"

"She handed it over. A defense lawyer might question where she got it, but it's different. Is there anything interesting?"

I scanned the PDF and shrugged. "Not much we don't already know. I'll summarize this too, and then we can decide what to do with the records."

No more delay. Time to see what the cops really had on Joan. I would have to check with Rance to make sure he got the copy Paul promised. Another example of not letting go, I guess. But really, I only needed the notes to help the case; Rance would need the files to defend Joan if we failed.

I pulled out my phone and opened the file we'd set up for our investigation. "The same cops signed the documents on all the new files. Does that mean anything?"

He was watching me rather than reading. How long had he kept the file before he let me see it?

He nodded toward the pages. "If they aren't corrupt, they know who is. I did check, and the signatures are legit."

I flipped a few more pages and added more names to the list on my phone, taking pictures of the new documents. Paul didn't stop me. I took the last photo and closed the folder. "Lots more details, but nothing popped out at me," I said.

"It strengthens the idea that cops are involved, if not the perpetrators. You done with this so we can start looking at it together?"

"Why are you so sure? Or why aren't you pushing me in

another direction? Like Zoe said, shouldn't you be holding the blue line?" If he wanted me to trust him, he should stop being so suspicious.

"I'm not the kind of cop who thinks the uniform or badge gives you a free pass."

29

I refilled my bowl with leftovers and ate while I thought it over. I wasn't hungry any longer, but I couldn't resist the last few bites. Maybe I should make Paul my Chinese food buddy. The food didn't resolve anything, and it was time to start planning next steps. If this case involved crooked cops, I wanted it solved before I found myself with a pile of tickets for imaginary violations.

"Should we go back to my place to plan?" I asked as the server cleared everything but our teacups.

"We're fine here until they close," Paul said. He talked to the server and within minutes we had a fresh pot of tea. "They won't come over again unless we call."

"I thought you didn't get special attention as a cop."

"Not because I'm a cop; because I eat here a lot."

"And the jaywalking ticket?" I don't know why I couldn't just believe him, but my gut insisted he was hiding something.

"True, we did cross illegally, but they didn't try to ticket the other four people who crossed before us. I can write you up if it would make you feel better." He grinned at me, and I was sure he'd pull out a book of tickets if I said yes.

"I'm fine. I agree it was targeted. So where do we go from here?" I had some ideas; I wanted to hear his first, because he might have some cop-way of solving it.

"Before I tell you, I want to know what your goal is here."

"To get the bad guys." Why was he asking? "And I guess to avoid being framed myself."

"Is that what Rance is paying for? I'm not being an ass, Charity. If we have different goals, we'll screw things up."

Maybe this was what my gut was trying to tell me. We could be about to butt heads on the most important part of the case. But he knew what I'd agreed to with Rance; anything else was a side benefit. "What's your goal?"

"Do you ever answer a question?" He held up his hand when I started to argue. "No. It's fine. My goal is to catch the dirty cops, if they are behind it. If you just want proof of a frame-up, then we part ways at some point."

I'd been so focused on catching the killer as a way to prove Joan innocent that I hadn't given a thought to there being other outcomes. And I had my own other outcome to pursue: I wanted the killer. Just getting Joan off the hook wasn't enough if no one investigated Kingston's murder.

"Fair enough. I want the killer. I know there's probably a way to prove the frame-up without another suspect, but I don't want that. If it's cops, then I want them. If it turns out not to be cops, I still want the killer. Rance didn't tell me to get her off the hook, and he's ready to accept she is the murderer and still defend her."

I'm not sure how that all boiled out of me. I did know it all before I spoke, but the force of it was a surprise.

"Okay. If it turns out to be someone other than the cops,

I'm still helping you. But the priority is to catch or clear the police for me."

He stared at me, probably looking for evidence of a lie, but I was happy to get on board with this approach — and not just because I was tired of poking around randomly.

"Okay, where do we start?"

"We'll look through this file together and talk about all the names. We have to keep in mind that this could be two separate crimes, not just one scenario where the person who killed Kingston also framed Joan."

"If it turns out to be that, I'll take the frame."

"And you'll find the killer behind our backs?"

How did he know me so well? "I was kind of hoping we could make our partnership official. Not that I want to work with the VPD again, but maybe you and I could solve this murder?"

"We'll see. I won't let a killer go free, Charity, but I can't let you work a murder without authorization."

Something to deal with if it came up. For now, I stuck with the idea that the killer framed Joan. I pulled out my phone to take notes. Paul put his pad on the table and opened the shared file.

We went through every page of the file. I took more photos and Paul added information to the spreadsheet. It took a couple of hours before we decided there was nothing more to glean.

"I think we've found the cops," I said. "This Evelyn Moore, isn't she the one who accused you?"

"Old problem, Charity. Probably no connection."

"So Bill Walker, Chris Bracken, and maybe this Lucy Valette, then. Any idea who might be running them?"

"It could be Jackie or Vince," Paul said. He tidied the

pages back in the folder then placed it in his briefcase. "You want another tea?"

I'd been drinking water while we worked. "No, I'll need to make a quick stop before we go."

Paul called for the bill while I ran to the restroom. When I got back, he was paying.

"I can expense this," I said.

"Don't worry. My treat. I love introducing new customers. I know you've been here before, but this is different from the usual dinner. New people keep him in business. I don't want to go looking for a new place to eat."

"Okay, thanks. I'll need you to order the next time I come, and I'll pay." I checked my phone. It was after midnight. "Should we get back together later in the morning?"

"How about now, and then I can drop the file back before it gets too busy at the station."

We were both energized by finding a solid lead. Maybe we couldn't put our finger on a single driving force, but I was as sure as Paul that these cops were corrupt and would tell us who ran them if we put them in the right situation.

The walk back to my place was uneventful. The drunks were still poisoning their livers and the usual homeless people were turning in, either commandeering a doorway or headed east to one of the tent cities. More cop cars patrolled, but none paid any special attention to us.

30

David came down the stairs to greet us when we slipped in. I sent him back to bed so he wouldn't get involved in the discussion. I liked to think he was disappointed, but I wasn't sure he was completely awake. Like his instincts told him someone was in the house, and that there was no threat. When he first slept over, he'd jumped out of bed, gun drawn at the sound of a seagull landing on the patio.

My phone rang as I was clearing space for us to work.

"Vince?" I wasn't expecting him to call with anything useful at this time of night.

"Joan got a message to me," he said. "Stay away from her pet cop."

"How did she know?" I hoped Zoe didn't leave us and go to Joan in jail to whine about getting caught.

"Not the point. I passed on the message, now I'm going back to bed." He ended the call.

Paul was looking at me with a question on his face. I told him what Vince said.

"You knew she was going to interfere, right?" he asked.

Knowing it and dealing with the reality of it weren't the same thing. I was too tired to talk about it, and really there wasn't anything Joan could do about it right now.

"I suspected. But if Zoe went running to her, can we trust she'll turn herself in?"

"We'll still give her the chance." Paul lifted his briefcase. "I've got to get this back. If we're right, then anyone involved will be checking to make sure the proof isn't in the wrong hands. Maybe more now that Joan knows what's going on. So let's get started."

"I should probably get some sleep soon," I said. "One more look through now that we have the laptop. Make sure the shared files are available and I can continue alone."

"No more secret visits to suspects, Charity," Paul said. The look on his face reminded me of my middle school teachers when I kept asking questions they didn't want to answer.

"I meant when I wake up and until you're ready." He didn't seem to notice I hadn't agreed. "There is something I need to know about how the hierarchy works. I can't imagine a rookie cop or two could keep this plot going, or even get it started."

He opened the file on my table and told me to bring up the shared file. "Did we add the ranks of the cops we identified?"

I checked the column beside the names. "Some of them, but not all."

We spent ten minutes adding the information. Some from the files where most of the cops had provided the information, and some from his memory.

"Is it a clue? The ones who didn't add their ranks?"

Paul shook his head and continued to review the

column. "We all forget on days when we have a hundred or more things to sign. And some of the signatures we couldn't read might have the rank included in the chicken scratch."

There were a few signatures that I thought were simply doodles, but Paul assured me that the cops in question always signed that way. Seemed to me a bad idea, because if a crooked cop or even a criminal got hold of it, they could easily copy it. But maybe that was true for all signatures.

"You're right," he finally said. "What's going on needs a level of authority. What's been signed, or faked, isn't accessible to every rank. And some of this is only possible if a staff sergeant or higher is involved."

"We don't have anyone like that."

"It means we still have names to find. If we can grab one of the conspirators, we can turn them. It would be nice to work it out before we arrest anyone."

If we didn't get the person in control of the gang, they would get away. I didn't need him to tell me that.

"Okay, you have any ideas who to look at first?"

He turned his gaze to me. "I'm afraid to start looking, to be honest. Not physically afraid, but what if it's someone I like? Someone I respect. Whoever it is, they've managed to hide their real activities long enough to rise to command level. That means decades as a cop. Even if it's not someone I know, every case they touched comes into question."

"So, we should let them keep going?"

He rubbed his eyes and glanced at the laptop screen again. "No. The consequences are not our problem. Catching the asshole is."

"What rank do we start with?"

"You don't do anything until I can figure out a plan, right?"

"If you think I'm going to step back and let you finish this, forget it. Sideline me and I'll do this without you."

"I don't know how David sleeps so well with a girlfriend so determined to get herself killed or thrown in jail."

"I don't sleep all that well when people are talking in the house," David said. "Can I come down and get coffee?"

"Yes," I called back up to him. He'd probably heard everything we said. He'd tell me what I needed to know when Paul took off.

"Like I was saying, staff sergeant is the lowest rank, but maybe this is coming from higher up. Let me get some intel before you start digging. Please, Charity."

"Give the guy a break," David said. "You both need sleep. Take a few hours and then get back to it. Paul can get you the list, and even if he can't, a few hours of rest will help you think clearly."

I wanted to argue that I could go for hours. But I couldn't lie, the thought of bed shoved everything else out of my head. Just because I agreed to wait didn't mean I'd sit on my hands until Paul called. Our shared files held a ton of new material for me to pick at.

"Okay. Can you send me the job descriptions or whatever the VPD calls them? I won't go asking questions; I just want to get a clearer view of what authority fits with each role."

"Fine. I'll pull a copy and send it when I return the thing." Paul pushed 'the thing' off the table into his briefcase. "Get some sleep."

He said goodbye to David and trudged out to the finger dock. I hadn't noticed his fatigue earlier, but I hadn't felt mine either. We'd both reached our empty tank stage.

"Come up to bed. I don't need to get up for another

couple of hours." David put his arm around me and pulled me close.

"But you wanted coffee."

"I wanted you guys to stop working."

31

I slept for four hours. Not enough, but my brain wouldn't stop working, so I decided to get up and use the ideas it kept tossing into my dreams.

The biggest idea I had was to look at the details of the other cases connected to our suspects. Not to see what they signed, or really anything about the people. I wanted the crimes.

Coffee and toast beside me on the table, I tried to log in with my credentials from the Hargreaves case because I thought there might be some other details Paul was holding back. It just felt like rereading the same documents wouldn't reveal any new leads. My credentials had been revoked. Stupid efficient security.

I started rereading the copies we made. At first, I just read trying to absorb the information differently than last time. Focusing on the whole file, not just the signatures or times. The second time through I made notes.

There was a commonality in the incidents. Not just that they were crimes, or that they were a particular crime. Not the times of day, arresting officers, locations. There was a pattern; I just couldn't firm it up in my mind. And it was going to take too much time to identify it without at least feeling sure that it would help.

I saved my notes, hoping Paul might see what I couldn't, and started on the second annoyingly brilliant idea I'd woken up with. The police report was not the only record of the crimes. Media articles, crime bloggers, and commenters on both publications might swing up a connection.

I'd been at it for hours without a break. I didn't want to stop to eat but I needed something to keep me focused. I put my plate in the sink and made another pot of coffee. I was in for a dive into the muck of internet trollery; I needed fuel.

I'd made the first few searches and was opening links in separate tabs when my phone rang: Paul. I looked at the time. How was it one o'clock already?

"Charity, I have bad news."

My heart stopped. Something had happened to David. I lived with that theoretical possibility every day. He was a cop, and it was a dangerous job. But bad news from any source sent my thoughts the same way every time. Theory was one thing, reality another altogether.

"Zoe," Paul said.

Not David, which was good. "She didn't turn herself in?"

"No, she's dead. Happened on shift last night. I don't know if it's connected or not."

We'd both agreed she wasn't part of the frame, but maybe we'd been wrong. "How?"

"Car accident is the official word so far, but I'm guessing murder."

"Where are you?"

"Getting the rank job descriptions like I promised. I figured it would be easier to get them legitimately than risk getting caught stealing them. The report of her death came in a few minutes ago."

Stealing was an exaggeration. "I need to see the documentation you have on her accident. If this was retaliation, we killed her by giving her time. And it could have been Joan issuing the order because we talked to Zoe."

"No, she's not that stupid. It's not our fault. If it's an accident, it would have happened or not, no matter what we did. If it's murder, we couldn't have triggered it because it would have to be planned. Zoe's killer is guilty, not us."

If it was murder, it was triggered by us talking to Zoe, regardless of whatever spin Paul tried to put on it. I didn't say it, because we were just wasting time when I could be looking at the details and making my own mind up. "I need to see the investigation."

"Come down here, to the station. I'll have copies of everything. No one will be suspicious if I have it. When one of us dies, it's all hands on deck."

"That's great for you," I said. "What legitimate reason would you have to show it to me?"

"I'll think of something," he said. "How long before you get here?"

"Half an hour. I'll call a cab." I ended the call, stuffed my laptop in my bag and ran upstairs to shower and dress in record time.

I wasn't prepared to believe this was a coincidence. I didn't think Paul was either, but how openly could he talk when he was surrounded by other cops?

Ten minutes after I went up, I ran back down the stairs, grabbed my phone to call a cab and noticed two missed calls, both with voicemails. David and Leigh, telling me a cop had died. Neither of them knew about our confrontation, but they'd be out of touch for as long as it took to get to the truth.

I wanted to call them both back and spill the details, but I couldn't. The only person I could talk to was Paul, someone I hadn't even liked up to a few days ago. Someone I wasn't sure how far I could trust. I sent a text to both David and Leigh to say I got the messages, and I was sorry, carefully leaving out why I was sorry.

The cab dropped me outside the station on Cambie and Second Avenue. The shadow thrown by the bridge seemed to sit on my shoulders as if it was pressing guilt into me. I kept up a mantra in my head that I was not responsible, and pushed through the door. The reception officer alerted Paul and I sat to wait for him.

Usually, the waiting area was quiet; people waiting for relatives to be released, or to make complaints, didn't usually get excited. The occasional drunk or high visitor brought noise and security into the space. Today, the only activity came from cops, moving across the floor or out to the street, determined looks on their faces, and not even a glance at the people sitting. Despite what Paul said, these people were investigating a crime, not an accident.

32

Paul laid the printouts of Zoe's case on the conference table. He'd booked a room on the admin floor to avoid being seen by his colleagues. I'd never been up here. It was quieter, and people seemed to stay at their desks more than in Homicide. I hoped he wasn't going to be in trouble for bringing me in, but it was late enough in the day for the early shift to be over. More people packed up and headed out as I watched.

"How did you get this so fast?" There were already more documents on the table than in Rance's file on Joan.

"Like I said, it's all hands on deck when a cop dies on the job. I told my boss I'd come in and help on my own time. We got this room so I won't get asked questions about other cases. And I can hide you up here."

"So, what exactly happened to Zoe?"

He pointed to a pair of reports. "The transcript from her radio transmissions and the attending officer's initial report."

The recording would be terrible at the point of impact.

The transcript was almost clinical. It started with Zoe's voice.

In pursuit of a gray sedan, plates obscured by mud.

Any make or model?

Nothing clear enough. This guy looks like he's been out mud racing, but it's not a pick-up so that's weird.

Heading?

East on Great Northern. Just passed Fraser Street intersection.

Then the transcription reported a scream, followed by the sound of a crash, followed by moaning. Then silence.

I wanted to ask so many questions, none of which were about hearing the recording. Paul shook his head and pushed the report from the first officer on the scene toward me.

The officer was Chris Bracken, a name we'd seen before.

He reported that the vehicle's driver, Constable Zoe Smith, had no pulse and appeared to be deceased. There was a faint odor of alcohol in the driver's area. The accident was a single car collision with a building. It appears Zoe lost control of her vehicle at high speed, crossed through the opposite lane of traffic, and smashed head-on into a Tim Hortons.

Another emotionless report of a horrific event.

"Is someone trying to find the car she was chasing?"

"We're requesting video from any cameras in the area. Her dashcam was disconnected. The building she hit has two, but they don't cover much of the road. There's a park across the street, so we don't have any Ring camera footage from residents."

"What's the policy on high-speed chases? What that Bracken guy reported reads like he's blaming her."

"Yeah, he is trying to make it all her fault. That she was

drunk on duty and behind the wheel. She didn't strike me as that kind of stupid."

I agreed with his assessment, but an autopsy would show the truth. Maybe given that she'd been caught and was probably on her way to jail, she'd had a few shots. "You didn't answer my question."

"The policy is not to engage in chases because of the danger to civilians, but you saw she was clear that they were the only vehicles. Policy is great, but when you get on the road, you have to make a choice."

"She didn't say why she was chasing the car."

"Yeah. That's a problem. Down there at that time of night? It's as bad as Marine Way. Long stretches of road and very few traffic lights."

"Will they do an autopsy?" I was getting a bad vibe from this information. Someone who was not a cop needed to get involved.

"Yes. I mean, they would anyway, but with Bracken's comment about smelling booze, they have no choice."

"Was anyone else involved?" It was pretty early in the case, but they must have made some headway.

"The next cop on the scene was Lucy Valette. Recognize the name?"

"From Joan's case. So, the two cops who showed up first are on our suspect list."

"Yeah. And they showed up really fast. Like they were waiting for the crash."

"Like one of them was driving a gray, mud-covered sedan? Someone needs to look for it parked on a side street."

"It's been too long," Paul said. "If you're right, they've had plenty of time to move it, wash it, and maybe crush it."

This goes way beyond framing a criminal or killing a thug. "Why? She wasn't part of the case."

He sorted some photos into order and passed them to me before answering. I couldn't tell if he was composing his thoughts or making up some bullshit story.

"We could be wrong. About everything. The Tiller case could be valid, and Joan's not being framed. Or if it is a gang of corrupt cops, Zoe could have been involved. Sometimes gut instincts are wrong."

"But if we aren't wrong?" I wasn't ready to go back to the beginning of the investigation. Yes, my gut could be wrong, but we needed proof of it before I just dropped my suspicions.

"Then soon we'll start finding evidence that Zoe killed Kingston and framed Joan."

I looked at the pictures. The car was mangled; she'd hit that building going a hundred. Something made her hit that speed. There were skid marks, so she tried to stop. What caused her to lose control?

"Who's in charge of the investigation?"

"Ted Johnson. He's a staff sergeant."

He held the rank we were looking for. Enough authority to steer an investigation in any direction he wanted. "And?"

Paul sighed and shook his head in resignation. "He's a nice guy. But he's also... I don't know if it's lazy or too trusting. He doesn't hold reins too tightly. He could be corrupt. Being a nice guy can divert suspicion for all kinds of bad behavior. Or he could be used as a scapegoat."

"Either way, we need to know who reports to him. Who he'd give too much rein or have as his second in command. Too many names in common, Paul. If this was a small-town force, that wouldn't be a red flag, but the VPD is huge."

33

W e just stared at the documents on the table. I didn't know what Paul was thinking, but I knew I felt cold radiating from my gut. I'd known we were probably right about the involvement of cops in this mess, but one of them was dead. Yes, Kingston's murder started my case, but this was different. The idea that people who were supposed to protect us from criminals were willing to kill one of their own had dropped a load of fear and rage on me. They had a lot of power, and I could just as easily be framed for a crime — even this murder — to get me out of the way.

"We can't let this go on," I said.

"No. I think we need to stop trying to find a suspect outside the station," Paul said. He opened his laptop and logged in to a page of organizational charts. "This is Ted's current reporting structure. I'll print it out and get us some coffee. We're going to be here until we connect some dots."

He logged out and left me alone. I pulled out my laptop and brought up the list of suspects we'd created. We needed to use a crime board. I could imagine Paul's objections if I asked, but pulling a theory together on a laptop screen wouldn't cut it. I scanned the folder of pictures I'd taken of Rance's journal. Nothing jumped out at me as helpful, and Paul was right: I'd tainted the evidence.

The PDF of Zoe's notes was in the same folder. I opened it to see if I could find anything that would have triggered her murder. She hadn't listed any names or accused anyone of murder. I'd let Paul figure out if he could use the information. Maybe as a bluff, if we ever caught a suspect.

When he returned, Paul had a sheaf of papers under his arm, two mugs of coffee in one hand and a carafe in the other. He placed everything on the table and pulled a stack of sticky notes out of each pocket.

"We need to be very careful how we do this," he said. "We can't put up photos or use real names in case someone comes by, but we need to put our data on the wall."

If the room had blinds, we could get some privacy, but it didn't, and we'd be better off seeing someone approach than being surprised.

"I put the names in the spreadsheet when we identified them," I said. "We can replace them with fake ones, or give them codes or numbers."

He tossed me half of the notes. "Assign codes, and I'll dig out what we need from the org chart."

It took just under an hour for us to cover the wall with notes. We had seven names coded. Six of them were cops, and we added Jackie Tomasino after hashing out whether we could ignore him or not. He was in jail, but that didn't mean he couldn't issue orders. And someone in the local criminal world must be involved. I convinced Paul that Joan's name should be up there too, even if he thought she wouldn't order Zoe's death.

"What else can we get from the system?" We'd dug

through Ted Johnson's recent activity, but he was definitely a hands-off leader. That didn't mean he wasn't running a gang of corrupt cops.

"I can't get into all the databases," Paul said.

"What about Joan's arrest history? It would be better if we had the actual files, but you gave them back."

He typed something and then sat back. "It's been restricted."

That was new. "Any reason?"

"It just says restricted. Maybe they think she ordered Zoe's death?"

"Or maybe there's a clue in her files that leads us to the facts." I pulled up the photos I'd taken of the documents and dragged a pad of sticky notes to my side. "Not the most efficient way to go, but I'll start reading."

He grunted and started typing more queries into the laptop. I desperately wanted to try my hand at it, but he'd been quite clear I was not allowed to touch his equipment.

"Whose signature is this?" I asked. The form was a five-year-old arrest document.

Paul moved the cursor to mark his place and looked over. "Ted's, I think." He leaned closer. "It could be someone signing for him. How did we miss that before?"

We hadn't been looking at Ted. I didn't say that, but pointed to the line above the signature. "This isn't on any of the other records. *Acknowledge amendment*."

He scanned the photo. "It happens, but there should be something crossed out and amended. The original is always kept. Hang on."

He opened another query and pulled up another copy. "This is from his earlier career. See the signature? It looks like he was rushed on yours."

"Or it was in a pile of other documents, and he didn't

know what he was signing." I could see the connections starting to rise out of the mess. "This was taken by Evelyn Moore. It's a statement from Jackie Tomasino."

Paul stopped reading his screen. "What was the charge?"

"Joan was arrested for possession of unregistered guns. Jackie's statement reads like he saw her load the weapons into her trunk. Well, it does now. He hasn't signed the amendment."

"Send me the photo and I'll print it."

He brought back two copies of the printout. One he put aside, and the other he started circling parts. When he finished, he gave it to me. "The circled stuff is fishy. In the best light, Evelyn forgot to get Jackie's signature, and Ted was slammed with work when he signed the document so he didn't check. Joan was arrested but not charged, so the file was closed."

I didn't believe this was a series of innocent mistakes. "Or, Jackie gave Evelyn the information she needed to arrest Joan. Evelyn forged Ted's signature or hid it in a pile of other forms he was signing."

Paul nodded. "Or Ted found the statement from Jackie and edited it before signing it because he was busy. Then the case fell apart, so he didn't get a chance to tidy up the loose ends, like Jackie's signature."

"We need to know which scenario is right," I said. "We focus on three people? Ted, Evelyn, and Jackie?"

Paul looked at the wall of notes and then at the signature on the arrest record. "Yes, from what we've found, these are the three most likely people in charge of this frame-up, and probably a lot more. Fuck. I thought we'd find someone on the force being used by a criminal. Now that I see all this, my experience tells me Jackie isn't in control — or he recently lost control to a cop."

34

Paul reached for the carafe of coffee and poured himself a mug. He took a gulp and then spat it out. Okay, into the mug, not on the floor. "Cold."

"That happens," I said. My stomach was sour from all the caffeine. I checked my phone. We'd been here for six hours. I hadn't noticed how long we'd been sorting through the information. The people who worked on this floor would be heading back to their desks in a couple of hours. "I'm surprised there's any left. It's getting early. Should I be here when the day shift starts?"

"I'll get us some water," Paul said. "We can still work for an hour before we need to clean up and head out."

I nodded and waited for him to leave. He'd forgotten to log out of the system. Or he trusted me not to look while he was gone. Idiot.

I did an employee search and the personnel file opened. He'd lied about not being able to get it. I didn't have enough time to read much, but I wrote down the contact number for Evelyn. Paul might have some difficulty deciding which cop was in charge, but I was sure this Evelyn person was in the right position to manipulate her boss and a handful of patrol cops. I exited out of the system and grabbed my phone.

She worked the day shift, and unless she was calling in sick, Evelyn might be up and getting ready. I wanted to set up a meeting. If I talked to her, maybe I could find a way to prove to Paul she was guilty. Or that we should move on to the next name.

All I got was her voicemail. I ended the call because... well, I hadn't prepared to leave a message, and Paul walked back into the room.

He placed two glasses of water on the table and stood there staring at me.

"What?"

"You look like I caught you doing something wrong."

I blamed it on the fact I was strung out from too much coffee and not enough sleep. It takes energy and focus to get away with anything. "I'm just tired."

He sat. "I've been a cop a long time, Charity. Who did you call?"

I could feel my face going red. "Maybe I was checking in with David."

"But you weren't."

I wasn't going to get out of this with bluster. "I called Evelyn Moore's cell number."

Everything about him tightened up. For a second, I thought I saw fear, but he was probably just trying to control his anger.

"I didn't leave a message."

He still didn't relax.

"I used my phone, not this office one."

He rubbed his face with one hand then took a deep

breath. "Okay, at least you didn't accuse her of anything. How did you get her number?"

"You left your computer logged in."

"Fuck. I was hoping it was some PI thing. If you got into her personnel file using my login, there's a record."

The coffee in my gut churned. "Is it going to alert anyone?" If I'd gotten him in trouble, I would do everything I could to fix it.

"No, but if she gets suspicious, she can ask for a privacy report. And if we end up arresting her, the defense lawyer can ask for everything in her file. It's very likely she'll know, but if we're lucky it will be after she's arrested."

We could still investigate until she tried to stop us, and maybe Paul would be safe. "Okay. That means we need to work fast, right? Catch her before we get sidetracked with a complaint."

"First of all, remember we don't know she's the one who framed Joan."

"And killed Kingston," I said.

"We don't know the same person committed both crimes. Hear me out, Charity. You called her cell, which leaves a record of your number on her phone log."

"She didn't have a home phone number, and I made sure to block my ID first." As I said the words, I realized I didn't remember doing it. I was in a hurry to get through before Paul came back. Blocking my ID only took a few taps, but did I remember? Fuck! Not something he needed to know right now.

"She's a cop." He waited for me to get some clue from his statement.

I hated this working together thing. I'd obviously forgotten something, but trying to sort through all the rules and shit about her being a cop wasn't easy on a caffeine-addled brain.

"Yeah, I'm sure it's going to make it harder to catch her, but if she's guilty it won't matter."

"Blocking your number means nothing. She can trace it easily. She shouldn't, and if she's innocent she won't try. If she's our criminal, she won't care about the rules. She'll just trace the call."

"And she won't just shrug and write it off as a wrong number?"

"She'll be on alert for anything odd right now."

I'd screwed up. "How do we fix this?"

"Let me take care of it, but you need to stop going behind my back."

"And you need to tell me more. I keep trying to solve the case. I'm just doing what I'd normally do. You keep holding back or taking too long to get information."

"You don't need to worry about making a case," he said. I'd gotten to him, though, because the words came out through clenched teeth. "You don't have to keep a nosy, obstinate, annoying civilian from getting killed."

"You don't need to protect me. I can do this on my own from here out. Finish your vacation and I'll let you know how it works out." I shoved all the papers we'd spread out into my bag and started pulling sticky notes from the wall.

"You can't," Paul said, his tone flat. "This is too deep for you to get anything to prove a crime, let alone find the criminal. You need my access, so you stick with my rules."

I spun around to yell at him. The look on his face stopped the words coming out. He was scared. For me? Or for his career? He was right, but I couldn't say that. I wouldn't be able to get any information from the police without him. And if Evelyn came after me, I would need his protection. I really should think before I act, but it was never going to happen. I guess I could see how he thought I'd betrayed him.

I turned back to the wall and pulled the remaining notes off. "I need to work alone for a bit."

"How?"

For someone who just said he was expert at reading people, Paul had no clue. "I'm not running off to do my own investigation. I need a bit of time."

"Let's hope Evelyn Moore gives you time." He held open my bag so I could drop the notes inside.

35

I got home just as David was getting up for work. What I should have done was crawl into bed for a couple hours of sleep, and to get over the fight and own up to my mistake. I just tossed my stuff on a chair and poured a big glass of water.

"What happened?" David asked. He nodded to my glass.

"Too much coffee already. I can't talk about the rest of it." I pulled some bread from the fridge and dropped it in the toaster. "I'll make breakfast, you get ready."

It wasn't much of a diversion, but if he stayed, he'd notice my mood. Since I couldn't tell him about the case, I didn't want to tell him about the fight. And I'd leave it to Paul to explain how stupid I'd been.

I also needed to guzzle a few glasses of water to dilute the caffeine in my system because my hands were shaking, and I was getting a coat of cold sweat on my skin.

David is a very smart man. He turned around and headed up to the shower. My main plans were to get back on social media, and to find a way to talk to Jackie in jail. One of those things would help me narrow down my search to one of the two people I was sure killed Kingston. My gut was telling me Ted Johnson knew what was going on. If he wasn't the killer, then he knew who was.

Jackie must've been pissed that he was in jail. He seemed to believe he was untouchable when we met. So he'd probably enjoy a visit from someone he could vent to about betrayal and revenge.

I pulled out the papers while I waited for our toast. Until David left, I wouldn't start placing them around the wall in the other room, but I could organize them into stacks.

There was an answer in all the bits and pieces we'd collected, and maybe I could solve this before Paul could arrest Evelyn or Ted. Or I might find something that proved they were not using their authority to threaten people and commit crimes.

I needed to find a way to connect the different papers to each other. That was the benefit of a murder board. It wasn't so much the details you had, it was how they linked, and sometimes how they didn't. There could be a huge hole in our logic that would only show when we analyzed all the data points.

"Looks like you had a productive night," David said. He'd come down while I was fantasizing about beating Paul to the solution. He'd stayed far enough away that he couldn't read the notes.

"It does feel like we have everything we need."

He buttered his toast while his pod of coffee brewed. "What does Paul think?"

He knew something was up. "Hypothetically, we agree. But I can't talk about it."

"What did you do?" He said it with no judgment, but there was no arguing he'd read my guilt right.

"We had a disagreement about methods. I needed some time alone."

He ate his breakfast while watching me sort papers into piles. I could almost hear his mind working out how to get more details out of me. I didn't know why he was so concerned. Paul was on vacation, so it wasn't like they'd run into each other at the office.

"You should make it up to him."

"Why do you assume I was the problem?"

"You won't make eye contact with me. You dodge my reasonable questions, and you needed time away from someone who is your best resource for the case. I'm a cop, remember?"

I couldn't tell him details without going into the case. Yes, I knew I could make up names to protect the guilty, but if I screwed up the NDA rules I might end up making it impossible to prosecute the real killer.

"Yes, I took an action that he didn't like. We needed to move forward, and he is way too cautious."

"And you took your action after a reasoned and articulate discussion." That should have been a question, but it was a statement. I chose not to rise to his sarcasm.

My phone rang, saving me from having to come up with an answer.

A number I didn't recognize. At this point I was happy to take a spam call rather than continue talking to David.

"If you don't stop, I'll make sure your boyfriend gets hurt bad, and your girlfriend at the VPD too."

The call ended. Had I remembered to turn on the recording app? I checked and there it was. Whether or not it was enough to help someone track the call, I had no idea.

"I have to go, Charity. The death of one of our own is

going to take all of us working long hours. Do you need me to mend fences?"

Thank God he didn't ask about the call. I hated actually lying to him, but I needed to digest the threat before I decided to act.

"I can do that," I said. "You might not even see him today."

"Okay, so it's just Paul? You didn't piss off anyone else?"

How did he know to ask that? Probably cop training.

"Paul and I will deal with everything. Be safe at work, and find Zoe's killer. It wasn't an accident."

He frowned like I'd said something important. I told him to be safe every time he left for his shift. He had a dangerous job. It was nothing to do with the threat. The suspicion I read on his face was all in my imagination. Or I'd let something drop about Zoe that I shouldn't know.

"You too," he said. Then he rinsed his plate and cup and placed them in the sink. "If you need me to stay away tonight so you can keep your murder board up, just let me know."

I walked him to the door and kissed him goodbye. Then I watched him until he was through the security gate for good measure.

Back in my house, I opened the door to the little living room and started putting notes up in preparation for a deep dive.

When they were all attached in loose groups, I sat on the couch with my notebook and a pencil, staring at the information.

36

I woke up with a start at the sound of a crash. The crash turned out to be the sound of my notebook hitting the side of the coffee table on its way to the floor. So more of a dull thud. I didn't remember falling asleep, but there were no notes in my book.

Apparently, it is possible to fall asleep while vibrating from a caffeine overload. The sun was fully up and the traffic on Georgia hummed dully in the background. A couple of words from a conversation on the boat moored behind me floated past. It was mid-morning, by the feel of it. I ran upstairs to use the bathroom and brush my teeth. During the nap, my subconscious had been hard at work. Nothing about the case, just two truths about me. I was an asshole to Paul, and I should warn David and Leigh about the threat. And, I guess, a third: I made very poor decisions when I was tired and buzzing.

I changed clothes after a quick wash and texted Leigh and David, saying we needed to talk.

David responded immediately with a time that they

would be together in private. I had thirty minutes to prepare.

Back in the living room, I stared at the wall, waiting until David called. Still nothing that looked remotely like proof. We needed to get answers.

My phone rang and I put it on speaker so I could move around while we talked. The guilt about keeping the threat secret made me antsy.

"So, what do you need to say?" Leigh asked.

There was no way to warm up to this, and they were both working on Zoe's case, as far as I knew. "I got a call this morning. A threat."

Silence. I had to force myself not to fill the void. It felt like hours before David spoke.

"Why didn't you tell me this morning?"

"Who threatened you?" At least Leigh was keeping to the topic.

"Not me this time. I have to back off or you will both be hurt. Nothing specific, but Paul and I think... Damn, I can't say anything. If we are right, your careers might be in jeopardy."

"You must be close," David said.

"I can back off," I said. I mean, it's the last thing I wanted to do, but Paul could take the case from here. He would give me the evidence I needed for Rance.

"Don't you dare, Charity," Leigh said. "We can take care of ourselves."

"Paul will warn us if it gets risky," David said. "Now that we know, there are steps we can take to protect our reputations."

Wow. They really had confidence in me. But that came with a lot of responsibility. If I screwed up, it would affect my boyfriend and one of my three best friends. "What do you mean by steps?"

"Don't worry about that," Leigh said. "Don't let whoever this is scare you off. We're adults, and we're cops. You need to be careful if someone feels powerful enough to keep threatening you."

"Do you know who it was?" David asked.

"Disguised voice, but probably the same person as last time. There was something about the way he or she spoke, the word choice, something that tickled my recognition."

"I can try tracing the call," David said. "Your cell, right?"

I didn't have much hope the call could be traced. "Yeah, my cell, but don't worry about it. Paul can try tracking it back."

"So, you plan to apologize?" David asked.

"Why do you assume I did something wrong? Maybe I've decided to forgive him."

They both laughed, like Paul was a rule-following saint and I was a troublemaking imp. Okay, that was exactly the truth, but they didn't have all the facts.

"Keep him close," David said. "If someone can threaten our careers, then you're in danger too. And you might not get a warning next time."

That sent a chill through me. "I'll call him when we're done. You both need to take care."

I sent a text to Paul, then scanned the walls for clues again while I waited for him to get back to me.

David was right about being careful. Cops had unions and lawyers. If whoever this was had the power to screw them, a PI would be no effort at all. They'd framed a criminal boss who had resources of their own. My license could be pulled because of complaints. I might find myself buried under nitpicky violations. That would hit Matthieu as hard as me. Val had Rance on her side, but she'd already been framed for murder once. Maybe not by cops, but they'd assumed she was guilty without even thinking about a frame.

All that added up to some stomach-churning stress and a conclusion. Only cops had that kind of power. We had five names that could fit the bill. Only two of them were positioned to control a gang. Our job was to find out if Ted was running the operation, or criminally stupid for not seeing what Evelyn was doing.

I was convinced that Evelyn was dirty, but without meeting her, I couldn't tell if she was conniving enough to get away with killing Kingston, framing Joan, and killing Zoe. And if Zoe wasn't part of the conspiracy, why did she have to die?

My phone pinged. Paul, returning my text.

Breakfast?

Food would make it easier to deliver an apology and suggest another probably stupid action.

37

He'd picked a restaurant near the station, so I guess he was prepared to head back there if we needed more data. It would be harder to hide me with everyone on shift, but maybe he had a ready excuse to be talking to a civilian.

He was sitting at a table in the back when I walked in. The place was busy. A few tables held cops in uniform and another two held men and women with the casual alertness I'd come to associate with detectives. It felt like a weird place for us to meet and discuss crooked cops, but I trusted Paul to know what he was doing. That was my new inner voice talking. The old one piped up with a sarcastic 'you, trust a cop? Yeah, right.'

Paul had already ordered coffee, and now that I wasn't buzzing with the stuff, I wanted more. "You have something?" I asked.

He pushed the laminated menu toward me and said, "Decide what you want. We'll talk when I'm sure we won't get interrupted."

His tone was flat. He was still mad at me. I'd have to deal

with that first. The server appeared, and I ordered my standard breakfast platter, hash browns, bacon and eggs, over easy, sourdough toast. I wasn't sure when I'd be able to eat after this since I was pushing to speed up the case, so I needed a solid base.

We sipped coffee and I watched Paul while we waited. He discreetly scanned the restaurant. I wasn't happy to sit with my back to the room, but he'd gotten here first.

"Anything interesting?"

"You saw the uniforms when you came in?"

"And the detectives," I said, to prove I was observant. "I didn't recognize any of them. And shouldn't they all be out trying to find Zoe's killer?"

He looked down at the cup he was holding in both hands. If he was trying to be casual, it was pretty awkward. Maybe it was just him getting his pissed-off-at-me under control before he said more than a few words.

"Cops work better if they get breaks, Charity. Exhaustion isn't the best state to make connections or important decisions. Anyway, the first table is Walker, Bracken, and Valette. They keep looking over."

When I said I hadn't recognized anyone, I'd meant the detectives. I'd glossed over the tables with uniforms and registered them as generic cops. A tingle ran across my shoulders at the thought I was being surveilled by three of our suspects. "Maybe they're wondering why we're together." It was weak. Two of those people had already tried to intimidate me.

"No, they know something is up. That's good. I picked this place because it's a hangout. It's making them nervous to see us together, and nerves will make them sloppy."

Great. And making them nervous could also make them desperate. I wasn't going to start an argument before I apologized for my last reckless act. Although maybe I'd rubbed off on him just a little. This wasn't the act of a cautious rule follower.

The food came; I dipped toast in the egg yolk and took a bite to reward me for what I was about to do.

"Two things," I said, after I swallowed. "Before we start digging again."

He lifted a spoonful of oatmeal. "Go ahead."

"I was stupid last night. I should have talked it over with you before I called her. I'm sorry."

He swallowed and nodded. Like he couldn't be bothered to accept my apology.

"Second, you could have warned me about this plan. I can't say I feel great walking into a nest of cops without notice."

He chewed on another spoonful and nodded for me to continue. What was he chewing? That stuff looked like he could just swallow it.

"I got another threat."

That got his attention back to me. He put his spoon down and wiped his mouth. "When? Did you record it?"

"This morning. Yes, I have a copy. I'll send it to you when we finish here."

"And? The threat?"

"Same voice as last time. This was really short, so I'm not sure what use the file will be, but they threatened David and Leigh."

"Do they know?" He stirred his oatmeal again.

I picked up a rasher of bacon and took a bite. At least my breakfast needed chewing. When I finished, I said, "Yes. I called both of them. They said ignore it and solve the case."

He waved the server over and held up his cup for a refill. "What do you think?"

"I hate it. But they can take care of themselves. And they have guns."

"So we continue. Good."

"Did you find anything?" I bit into a forkful of hash browns. It was his turn to update me.

"I got a log of the calls made from Johnson's phone in the last three weeks, and Moore's too. We can look for any incriminating numbers."

"You think they would make calls from their desks about criminal activities?" I couldn't believe either of them would be so stupid.

"Probably not, but we might see something else that points us to the next clue. I also got access to their financials. I've requested cell phone records too."

How did he get all that? "Don't you need a warrant for financials and phone records?"

"Not the desk phones. They're property of VPD. I have some friends who'll help get warrants when we need them. Nothing illegal, and it will stand up in court."

It sounded like he didn't want any more questions. "It's taking too long," I said. "We keep poking around looking for clues to clues. I think we need to take a different approach."

It was risky to take a left turn in the middle of investigating, but the only traction we got was when someone threatened us. Nothing we found really led to anything.

"You don't think it was a cop?" He sounded disappointed.

"I think it was one of those two, Evelyn or Ted," I said. "What I mean is we're too scattered. Rance hired me to prove whether Joan was framed or not. We're looking at a potential gang of crooked cops. We aren't focused, right?"

"I'm listening. You want to go back to look at the frame-up. Keep our attention on one crime."

"Sort of," I said.

I waited for the server to give us another coffee top up. When she left, I heard a lot of chairs scrape on the tiled floor. I turned to see all the uniformed cops headed for the door. Two of them made a point of looking right at us. I felt like running away through the back door. Then we were alone. The detectives had left a while back.

"Jeez, they're like high schoolers," Paul said. "How the fuck are they managing to get away with crimes?"

"They must be on a very short leash. Maybe we can turn one of them against the leader?"

"Not worth it until we have something to use as leverage," Paul said. "Was that your new idea?"

"No. We should focus on solving Kingston's murder. Every record about Joan is suspect, right? But Kingston's file might be clean. If we're right about the cops, then solving his murder should prove the frame job, and reveal the crooked cops."

38

Paul didn't disagree with my plan to go after one of the cops. But he'd refused to go after Ted or Evelyn without at least one more corroborating piece of evidence. In the spirit of atonement for my last mistake — not really a mistake — I let him have his way until I could come up with something better.

So now we were sitting in his car facing my local coffee shop and deciding how to proceed. We'd tracked the three cops we suspected of being part of the gang, but they could only be soldiers, since they had no authority to arrange arrests or releases.

One of them was sitting drinking a latte not five minutes from my home.

"So, do we pretend we just dropped in for coffee, or what?" I wanted to go drag him out and beat the information we needed out of him. Not that I could, but it felt great to imagine. My home was a safe place, and yet since day one of being a PI people had walked right up and through the door regardless of my wishes.

Paul scanned the area, and I followed his gaze. Not much

foot traffic right now. People were already at work and not yet coming for their mid-morning fix. The coffee shop was quiet. Bill Walker sat alone, facing the street. He was pretending to look at his phone, but he made no move to swipe to a new page or tap in a search. He was out of uniform, which was probably to our benefit. Hassling a cop in his blues would bring attention. Approaching him was risky enough when no one knew he was police.

"No. We'll be up front with our reasons. Maybe it will put him off-kilter; maybe his reaction will tell us something."

"And the fact that he seems to be watching the only street I use to exit the marina on foot?"

Paul unlocked the doors and released his seatbelt. "We'll hold that back. If we need to get aggressive, we can threaten him with stalking charges."

If I thought they would stick, or I wouldn't end up being more harassed than ever, I'd put the charges on every member of this underhanded little gang.

Paul led the way through the door. It worked for me. I'm not exactly a tiny woman, but he hulked. His entire body changed while we walked from the car. One step he was his normal, kind of casual self; the next he was an angry, powerful man. I would never be able to pull that off, but it didn't stop me from memorizing the differences.

This wasn't the first time I'd seen Bill Walker. He'd been one of the cops who tried to intimidate me in the station, and he'd been at the table when Paul and I met for breakfast. He was tall, thin but in that kind of wiry way, and he looked like he was in his mid-twenties, so not long in uniform. His hair was braided into a pattern on the top and cut in a fade at the side. So when he was wearing his uniform hat, the braids would be covered.

"Walker," Paul said, as he dragged a third chair from the next table.

I sat in the one across from Bill and leaned back, like I hadn't a care in the world. Although my stomach tightened, and my legs wanted to jump up and run away. It was scary how being caught between two alpha males could trigger primal instincts.

"Grewal." Bill wasn't going to volunteer anything; no emotions, no information.

"Long way from your usual hangouts," Paul said. "What's interesting enough to bring you down to Coal Harbour?"

Bill lived in Coquitlam, which was a good hour's drive from here, but he worked only a twenty-minute walk away. And Stanley Park was only a few blocks farther along, so he had plenty of legitimate reasons to stop for coffee here. Only one shady reason: to keep an eye on me.

"No rules against trying a new coffee place." Bill glanced at his phone again.

"There are rules against harassing citizens," Paul said. "Explain why you gave Ms. Deacon such a bad time when she was visiting Homicide. And when you threatened to give her a ticket for jay walking."

That was news to me. Was he also driving the cruiser that swerved away from stopping me? Or had I missed another attempt to irritate me off the case?

"Misunderstanding," Bill said. "At the station. I should have given her the ticket later, but I showed professional courtesy to you."

I was starting to think he'd have a good reason for why he did everything. Just enough to twist what I knew was the truth against me. Make me look like the asshole for bitching.

"You know Evelyn Moore?" Paul said.

I wasn't expecting such a bold question. Yes, we'd agreed to go in head-on, but what happened to finesse and interview techniques? Then I noticed Bill glance at his phone before answering. Was he recording us?

"Yeah, she's signed off on a few of my documents." Bill looked up after he spoke. His eyes slid over me and focused directly on Paul. "Why?"

"What's so interesting on the phone?" I asked.

"Game," he answered. Then he turned the phone to me, and I saw someone kicking a soccer ball. No sign of a recording.

"You do any work for her?" Paul asked, like I hadn't spoken.

"What kind of work? She sometimes assigns shifts, or picks people to work on task forces."

"You know exactly what kind I mean," Paul said. He leaned in toward Bill. "The kind that gets you in a jam you can't slide out of. The kind gets you fired with no benefits at best, prison at worst."

He looked at his phone again, but he wasn't focused on the action. He closed his eyes as he decided how to answer. Everything reinforced my belief he was guilty. He could deny everything, or say he knew the rumors that she was dirty and he had nothing to do with it. Or, and this one was unlikely in the extreme, he could break down and confess like Zoe did.

"There are some rumors," Bill said. "You should have heard them, but maybe it's just us uniforms who see it. She's dirty, right?"

"You tell me." Paul moved back out of his personal space.

"I don't do favors," Bill said. "Now leave me alone."

"She didn't send you down here to keep an eye on Ms. Deacon?"

Bill's eyes slid to mine again, and he shook his head.

Paul stood and tipped his head toward the door. "Let's go. We've given him his chance to get ahead of it. We'll move on to the next name on the list."

Bill went very still at that statement, but he didn't crack.

When we were on the street, Paul's phone alerted him to a text. "The call you got this morning came from a building downtown. It's a reception extension, so we're no closer to catching the caller."

"Fine, what next?"

"I'll pull the phone records for our suspects and we can go over them." He unlocked the car with his fob. "I'll see what other documents I can pull up. How about I come by in a few hours? I have a meeting to get to."

"Fine. Come to my place. I'll keep trying to find a reason to talk to the other people on our list."

"You don't need much of a reason," he said. "You want me to drop you off?"

"I'll walk." I watched him drive away and then headed for my place. My phone rang as I approached the gate. It was Rance, so I stopped and answered it.

"We need to meet," he said.

"Sure, when?"

"Now."

39

S omething about his tone worried me. Had he found his own proof that Joan should be released? Had Joan confessed? Was I in trouble? Of the three, I'd lay money on the last one. There was no point in arriving all sweaty from running, so I took my time. Well, I didn't dawdle, but I didn't hurry either.

I stepped off the elevator into the lobby of Rance's law firm. It was quiet, but at this time of day, everyone would be busy. A firm like this would make sure none of the hustle of the workers was apparent to the wealthy clients.

The receptionist escorted me to Rance's office. That was signal number two that I'd done something to piss him off. I knew the way and she'd waved me through before.

"Charity, have a seat," Rance said, pointing to the chair across from him. "I need an update, and I've heard a few rumors you need to clear up."

The nicest way of telling me someone had ratted on me that I'd ever heard. We must've been close if they were complaining to Joan's lawyer.

"We've got a few leads," I said. "Someone is definitely

messing with the records. We've pinpointed a few suspects and we're pursuing them."

"When you say 'we', you mean Paul Grewal is working with you as we agreed?"

Was that it? Was he about to kick Paul off the case? "Yes, only me and Paul. Is there a problem?"

"Not with that," he said. Rance looked at a notebook on his desk. He made a quick tick mark and then turned his gaze back to me. "Why are you investigating the police?"

Okay, so someone had indeed complained. "Because that's where the clues are. We think it's one of two people in control, and a handful of uniforms doing the dirty work."

He nodded and then closed the notebook, leaning his arms on the desk and pursing his lips like what he was about to say tasted bad.

"Look, we're close," I said. If I could stop him talking, maybe he'd listen to the facts. "If someone called you to pull us off the case, it could be the one we're looking for. Was it an anonymous tip?"

He held up a hand, so I stopped. Whatever this was, I'd listen and then explain.

"No one called from the police, Charity. It was Joan. You're treading on her business, and she's worried your actions will get her arrested for something she's actually done."

"Would that be so bad?" I regretted the words as soon as I said them. An investigator should be impartial when it came to clients. If they made judgments — or gave them voice — they wouldn't solve any cases.

"No, but I'd still be her lawyer. Like I said, I've heard rumors you're targeting police. And that you seem to be looking into more than a frame-up. Are you focused on the case we agreed to?"

Just because the call came from outside our suspect pool didn't mean it wasn't instigated by a suspect. I took the time I needed to stop the argumentative response. Rance was a client; he wanted his result. I couldn't get it any other way than by finding Kingston's killer. I sat forward and copied his pose, arms on the table, slight lean toward him. We were client and professional, not combatants.

"I am looking for the proof that Joan was framed. I believe she was, Rance. The woman is a pain in the ass, and she must make your job almost impossible, but she's not sloppy. If she killed Kingston, nothing would point to her."

"Glad we agree. So why are you investigating police corruption?"

That wasn't letting me off the hook, but we weren't fighting, so that was a win.

"It's easy to figure out she was framed, but you need proof. That investigation led us to the conclusion that there were dirty cops involved. When we started to look into it, I became a target of harassment — nothing big, don't worry — and threats. That means we're on the right track."

"So you find the proof of corruption, and then the person who framed my client confesses and she's set free. It's a big leap, Charity."

"Only if I'm wrong. And I'm not."

"You've sold me on finding the real killer," he said. "Police corruption is a giant pit of vipers. You could be right about them, and still not have the proof I need."

"Has something happened to move up the time line?"

"Joan is getting impatient. It's not great for her to be under suspicion. Her whole gang is being watched more than usual. That's fine from my point of view, but she's not going to let her people be taken down."

We were so close to identifying and catching the leader. I

couldn't let Joan's criminal empire get in the way. "Look, if we are right, we can push hard and get the leader of the crooked cops to make a mistake. A couple of days. If that doesn't result in freeing Joan, we can go back to the beginning. We won't have to, Rance. I am certain we will get what we need."

"Here's my concern, Charity. Even if you are right, investigating crooked cops is an internal matter for a reason. Say you catch this person; it might be months before they're pressured to confess. You will never hear the outcome, even from David or Paul. Joan could still go to jail for Kingston's murder."

"The cops won't have much interest in putting her back on the street, right? They want the corruption dealt with and screw everything else."

"I wouldn't put it that baldly, but essentially, yes."

"I'll find a way to get the confession," I said. I had no idea how to do that, but this was the only way to prove my theory.

"Something we can use to prove her innocence in Kingston's murder?"

"On a recording," I said. "I'll get whoever it is to tell me the story. I'll send it to you, and Joan can go back to petty criminal activities until she's caught for something she actually did."

He mulled that over for long enough that I started marshaling another argument.

"Okay. Keep focused on the frame job, Charity. I'll keep Joan from doing something stupid for a couple of days. Just don't get pulled into a corruption case. Or at least wait until Joan's free before you do."

40

I walked home thinking about our conversation. Rance hadn't actually said anything to make me suspicious, but the timing of his call was oddly perfect. While neither Paul nor I had recorded the names we suspected, it seemed as soon as we homed in on two targets, the pressure came from a different direction. Was it possible that Rance played a part in the corruption? Or was he being used by Joan to muddy the waters? Why would she do that? I had no answer for that. Who knew what went on in a criminal's mind?

A patrol car drove slowly beside me until I turned to look. Then the driver sped up and changed lanes. More intimidation? We'd pushed at Bill. It was possible he thought pushing back would get him off our radar.

He was stupid if he thought that. I guess some people — okay, most people — would avoid the notice of the police. I wasn't one of them. The more they poked at me, the harder I looked into them. If whoever was running this little gang wanted to deflect my interest, leaving me alone would be much more successful.

Another patrol car was parked a block away. Or maybe the same one. As I passed, someone inside hit the sirens, almost shocking me into a heart attack. Then the door opened and a cop I didn't recognize stepped in front of me.

"I need to see your ID," he said.

"Why?" I wasn't obliged to do as he asked. Just because I didn't recognize him didn't mean he wasn't part of the gang.

"We've had a report of a robbery suspect in the area. Fits your description." He didn't move.

"And you think my ID will prove I'm that person?"

"Just let me see your ID and you can go on about your day if you aren't our suspect."

"You have a name for this suspect?" I didn't say that the story was all bullshit, but it was. He could push it and take me in, but there was nothing to hold me on. I'd call Rance and get out with no charge.

"Just cooperate, please."

"No."

"Wait here," he said, and reached into the cruiser for his radio.

I heard him ask for confirmation about the criminal they were apparently looking for. Then someone responded, but I couldn't make it out.

He put the radio back and stepped aside. "The person is in custody."

I watched him get back in the cruiser and drive away. He wasn't in on the intimidation; someone had used him to hassle me.

The stress reaction started as soon as he was out of sight. My legs didn't want to hold me up. My heart raced, and I had trouble filling my lungs.

Adrenaline. I forced myself to keep walking because it was the only way I knew to burn it off. A few blocks to my turn off might not be enough, but I could keep going along the water. If Evelyn was recruiting regular, not-corrupt cops to help, it changed things. I needed to be more careful. If there was a car in the turnaround by the security gate, I'd continue to walk to the Bayshore and call every cop I knew I could trust.

I needed to decide about Rance. Was he a crooked mob lawyer, or a great guy who was very good at his job? If Rance was part of the corruption, then why had he called me in to prove Joan's innocence? I thought about all the help he'd given me and Val. He'd helped Val when she was falsely accused of murder. And he seemed cool with Val and Rory's relationship, even with Val's less than pristine past. There was no way he'd let them live in his pool house if there was a chance they'd find out he was on the wrong side of right.

This was draining me, and using up time I could be thinking about catching the person I knew was a bad cop. I moved Rance's name permanently off the suspect list. If he was involved, we would never catch anyone. The reason he put pressure on me was because Joan put pressure on him. Not orders from Evelyn or Ted.

I turned the corner from Georgia to Broughton; no black and whites lurking. The next block was pedestrians and bikes only, so if I was being followed, they would need to come down Nicola to catch up. It wasn't a great way to hide because there were only a few places I could be headed. What I decided to do was go to Cardero's for a nibble and a drink. A seat on the patio would provide a perfect view of the road and any stray patrol cars.

When I sat with the umbrella positioned to shade me, I opened my notebook on the table and started reviewing my notes. Not that I expected to get any new clues out of it, but I needed something to do. And it would be easy to note the numbers of any patrol cars.

The waiter placed my drink, a bloody Caesar, and my snack, tuna tataki, on the table and left me alone.

After ten minutes of pretending to read my notes and constantly glancing at the road to see if I was being stalked, I gave up. This wasn't getting me anywhere. Paul and I agreed that we needed to speed up our investigation a few hours ago, and we hadn't done anything.

I sent him a text asking how fast we could get going. It took him five minutes to answer.

On my way to your place.

I called for the bill and drained my glass. The tuna was long gone.

41

The phone records were laid out on the coffee table in my living room. I'd brought Paul in so he could see the setup. The information was still tacked to the wall, and David knew it was there, so he stayed out. Paul and I sat side by side on the couch and looked for connections in the call logs. Or, if not a clear link, a pointer to one of the people we'd selected as our prime suspects.

"If we had this in a spreadsheet, we could sort it. There are so many calls, it would be nice to sort out the incoming."

Paul just grunted and I decided to take it as agreement. No point in talking about it any longer; we had the data, we would deal with it. And if this was too easy, I wouldn't trust the results. Whoever was really in charge knew how the system worked. It was possible we'd find nothing. The calls showing the proof would be on burner phones.

"You have a copier?" Paul asked. "I don't want to mark up our only set."

I slid back a panel and turned on the printer. "Load them in and make two copies. I'll grab some highlighters."

I also pulled out a file folder to hold the originals. We

were in for a long session, and it would be helpful to keep ourselves organized.

"Do you have a gut feeling about anyone?" I asked, while my printer chugged out the forty pages for each set of duplicates.

"I'm leaning toward Moore," he said, not looking away from the printer. "She could be manipulating Johnson, and she would be closer to the patrol officers we know about. It could still be Johnson running the whole thing, but I've worked with him, and I can't see him being turned. Missing the clues that he was being used? Yes. But not actually being dirty."

"What about Rance? Do you think he might have a hand in?" I'd dismissed him, but maybe I'd been too quick to do it.

"MacDonald? Not a chance. He's a defense lawyer, but he doesn't win all his cases. And he's seen enough damage done by corruption that he wouldn't touch it. If he gets caught, he loses everything."

"So no chance we're dealing with something John Grisham might write about?"

"Nope."

The original documents went into the folder and then into my filing rack behind another sliding panel. "So, if we find someone making suspicious calls, what then? We need a stronger link between them, right?"

"I have a little more to use," Paul said. "I think we should start with the calls. I'll take Johnson's record and you take Moore. Highlight numbers that are called more than twice. Then we'll see if that tells us anything."

We split the papers between us. Paul wrote Evelyn's number on the top of his first sheet; I did the same with Ted's on mine.

I got why he didn't want to tell me his news up front. We

should look at the calls with open minds. If I knew something about either of them, I'd be looking for confirmation, not information. I didn't like it, though. It felt like he was holding back. Not in the logical way, but because he didn't trust me.

"How much would they normally communicate?" I asked, after I highlighted the twentieth call between them in two days.

"Hard to believe it's this much," Paul said.

I looked over and saw his pages highlighted with two colors. One matched mine, and the other didn't. "What else are you looking at?"

"Finish up your list and I'll tell you. I want to see if you recognize the pattern."

I bit back the annoyed words that came rushing to me. This was some kind of cop procedure, and I should shut up and give it a try.

Ten minutes later I shoved my papers to the center of the coffee table and looked at Paul. "Okay, what are we seeing here? All I have is a lot of calls between an employee and her boss."

"They work on the same floor; how much more contact would they have? It looks like Johnson is micromanaging Moore. He's way too hands-off to do that."

"So she's micromanaging him? How do we prove that?"

"I have the numbers for Walker and Bracken. Do you see a pattern?"

Only two of the cops we suspected of being part of this gang? "What about Valette?"

"I didn't have time to pull hers."

I scanned through his second set of highlighted lines. There was something, but I couldn't get it from just reading. I pulled out a sheet of the easel paper I kept under my printer. Having these cupboards built into the bulkhead of my home gave me lots of flexibility in shape and capacity. I used painter's tape to attach the sheet sideways on my wall so I could make a time line.

Paul let me work without comment and I forgot he was there as the pattern emerged. "One of them gets a call from Evelyn right after she calls Ted. Never after he calls her. She's issuing orders. I still don't know if she's just a relay, or she's in charge."

"Look at the records for two days ago. Right after we talked to Smith."

There were a series of calls from Evelyn's phone to Bill and Chris, and a third number. I asked and Paul confirmed it was Lucy's. By the duration of the calls, it seemed she was trying to track them down. Eventually, the call went through to the third number. It lasted three minutes.

A chill emanated from my spine. This couldn't be right. "She told this person to kill Zoe?" Even as I said it, I couldn't quite believe Evelyn would do that through the police phone. We weren't the only people who could get our hands on these records. "And no call to Ted."

"Evelyn Moore was a mentor in the academy when Walker, Bracken, and Valette went through. She recruited them before they even became police."

42

Not proof that the cops framed Joan, and I'd bet that it wasn't enough to get the four of them investigated yet. It wasn't a waste of time, though. We knew these four cops were working together. We had a clear indication they may have conspired to kill Zoe. And we no longer needed to figure out who was in charge. Ted Johnson might be in enough trouble to get him early retired, but I didn't think he had a clue about Evelyn's little gang.

"We have to find something more concrete as proof," I said. "I need to see the personnel files of all four cops. I need access to any recent arrests, I need anything and everything you can sneak out of the station."

Paul didn't look up at me. He was staring at the time line, frowning. If he was hoping it would suddenly reveal a different result, he was going to be disappointed.

"I didn't imagine it, Paul. You found it first." Second thoughts at this point could mean we lose any hope of closing the case. Or cases, since we were looking at Zoe's death as well as the frame.

"I know. I just need to process this. The idea that someone, a sergeant or a staff sergeant, would order a cop killed? It isn't an easy thing to accept."

"And it's going to be hard to convince anyone we're right without a lot more data."

"Just give me a second, Charity. I'm not saying we back off. I'm... I don't know, in shock."

Or worried that he'd end up alone at the hardest part? Maybe he was worried that I'd dump him if I could close my official case before he was able to charge the cops?

"I'm in to the end, Paul. As soon as we know enough to get Joan out from under the murder charge, we can both go full force on the corruption and murder."

He sighed and turned his gaze back to me. "When we do, the shit will fly everywhere. No one wants crooked cops on the force, but no one gets love for finding and prosecuting them, either."

"Yeah, I know. I'll face some retribution. It's not like the cops love me anyway. I'll probably lose Leigh as a source. I don't think she'll walk away from our friendship — I hope not. I can find more sources. I don't have that many friends."

"David is the one who'll face the worst of it."

"You want me to ask his permission to keep going? I can tell you exactly what he'll say: 'I can take care of myself Charity. Do your job'."

"Yeah. It's what I would say in his position. I wanted you to go into this fully aware of what could happen. I appreciate you offering to see it to the end, but not if it's going to be dangerous."

"I faced a Russian mob boss and a deranged hit man in the company of the Hells Angels. You don't think I can handle some pissed off cops? And the ones who aren't crooked will back off quickly. Or maybe not lash out at all." I didn't tell him about the incident earlier. It would distract him, and nothing bad had happened.

He grinned and held out his hand. "Okay. Partners."

I shook it, and then pointed to all the paperwork laid out on the coffee table and the walls. "This isn't enough. We're making connections based on incomplete input. I'm not saying we're wrong, but we can't expect to convince anyone unless we've eliminated all doubt."

"You're asking for a lot of things I can't access."

"Like the personnel files? Remember, I found Evelyn's number by just querying her file."

"Yeah. I kind of lied there. I can't get the full files without permission, but contact info is available to everyone. Not all of it. You wouldn't get any result on an address, or next of kin, or any complaints."

Complaints would move us a long way to getting proof. We could interview the person complaining, or witnesses, or something. I was getting frustrated with the way he still kept me behind a screen. Like he trusted me, but only so far. I wasn't a cop and didn't get that last bit of faith. "Paul, we're hamstrung on this if we can't go deep. Proof of corruption isn't going to be in a document any cop can access. You know that."

"It's not going to be in any document," he said. "It's going to be in the links between different documents. Neither of our suspects are smart enough to run a gang *and* stupid enough to leave evidence in the open."

"I guess so, but what can we do without it? Following someone, or more than one person, won't work. Whoever is calling in the threats to me knows we suspect a cop. Everything going forward will be hidden more deeply the longer we take to find it. We need proof from before they got good at covering their tracks."

"We can't do this at the station," Paul said. His voice was a bit distant. He was talking through how we would get what we needed, not saying how difficult it would be. "Here, I guess. You've got strong Wi-Fi, and maybe we can set up an untraceable connection. We'll use my laptop, so if someone tries to trace it, the first clue they get is legitimate."

"I already have untraceable Wi-Fi." It was a matter of some settings, and a device I put between the modem and my network. "It comes in handy sometimes."

"I need to get my laptop from the station. Give me two hours. I'll try to get extended access without tipping off our suspects."

It suddenly felt like we were about to arrest the leader of the corruption gang. I knew we had a lot of reading and analysis to do, but we'd finally stopped fighting against being a team. There was no way we could fail. "I'll order a pizza. You pick up some beer?"

"And I'll let David know he should stay away for the duration. The less he knows, the easier it will be for him to distance himself from the shitstorm."

43

W e squished together so both of us could read the screen on Paul's laptop. He wouldn't let me do any actual typing, and the screenshot feature was disabled, so I was forced to make notes by holding my notepad on my lap and hunching over to scrawl a few words.

Having all the information we needed at hand didn't mean the proof popped up as soon as we received the results of our first query. This was going to be about connections. I already had a thumbnail sketch of the key points in the personnel files. We knew Evelyn was mentoring the three uniformed cops, but no formal agreement showed up in anyone's records. Paul said it wasn't that unusual. Mentoring relationships could be informal. The best ones were. I didn't add that the worst ones were, too.

"There has to be a link between one of the cops and someone in the gangs," I said. "Search for documents that mention Jackie, Vince, or Joan along with any of our five suspects."

"Okay, I'll add Kingston to that search, too," Paul said as

he typed a string of letters and symbols. I'd been lucky the one time I searched the records. There was clearly some kind of cop coding for names and documents.

"What about Kingston's friends?" I asked. "Maybe the connection isn't direct."

"On the next search," Paul said. "If we put too many names in there, we'll get connections that don't move us forward."

The screen filled with links to various documents. Forty lines, but nothing to indicate there were more to come. "Start at the top?"

Paul clicked the first link. An arrest record for Kingston. Signed by Bill Walker, authorized by Evelyn Moore. Assault. Dismissed. It was a bar fight. Kingston was doing his job as a bouncer, someone got aggressive, and a fight broke out. The aggressor had a broken nose. Kingston suffered a bruised knuckle. The complainant withdrew the charge after he sobered up.

"We need to talk to that guy," I said. "Maybe he was convinced to withdraw."

Paul opened the next document. "Happens all the time, Charity. The guy probably wanted to hide the fact that he got so drunk he picked a fight."

I knew that, but we still needed to talk to the guy.

The next document and the five after it were similar. Kingston gets in trouble and the charge is dropped. All signed off by Evelyn, and involving Bill, Chris, or Lucy. That was too many for me to think it was legitimate.

"Is there anything in the list that will include Ted? We've got enough to conduct a few interviews, but we still don't know if it's Ted or Evelyn we need to stop."

Paul clicked and scanned the remaining documents. He gave me the name of the person charged or warned in each case. Kingston was never actually charged with anything. Lots of arrests, but not even one court date.

"Here," Paul said, bringing me out of my thoughts. "Ted signed off on releasing Jackie Tomasino for lack of proof. Didn't even go to the Crown to get the OK. It's done, but there's something else."

"What?" I poked him to express my displeasure at his dramatic pause.

"That's not Ted's signature."

I grinned at him. We'd found our first real clue. Something that couldn't be explained away. "Show me his real signature. Is there any way we can display his signature, this fake, and Evelyn's, all at the same time?"

"I can only display two side-by-side. If I do more, they'll be too small to compare." He took out his phone and took a picture of the screen. "I'll delete this as soon as we're done."

I nodded and waited while he pulled up several documents with Evelyn's writing. He picked one, and then found a bunch with Ted's. The two documents on the screen were clearly written by different people. Evelyn's writing was spiky and disconnected. Ted must have won medals for his penmanship. Her signature was similar to her handwriting, the first letter separate from the scribble of her last name. At least Ted didn't sign his name as though he was printing it, something old people did a lot. It was still a kind of scribble, but loopy rather than spiky.

Paul held his phone to the screen. The signature was a good try, and the basic idea was right, but Evelyn couldn't mimic the open, loopy structure. There were too many points on the top for it to be accepted as a good forgery. But if no one checked, then it would pass.

44

"We need Jackie, or maybe Vince," I said. "Someone to pull Evelyn into a trap. Or if not her, one of her lackeys."

Paul was busy typing queries and didn't answer me, so I kept talking. "If we figure out who is on her payroll, we can set up a meeting and record it."

He finished entering the request and turned to me. "I don't think going for Moore that way will work. She's likely to send someone rather than risk an in person meeting. And what makes you think Jackie will help us? Even if he's not working with her, he won't want to get on her bad side. And if he is, there will be retribution."

All good points, but I couldn't help feeling deflated. We had our answer and now we were stuck again.

"We go to Vince. He's got to be invested in freeing Joan. And we've got nothing indicating they're working together," Paul said. "We try to set up the meet between him and one of what you call Evelyn's lackeys, and work up to Moore."

Rance would have kittens if I didn't put Joan first. "We need to prove the frame-up. Use that to get Evelyn."

His laptop beeped. The screen was full again. Paul ignored it. "Getting Evelyn will clear Joan. Don't forget, Joan's not some innocent grandma. She runs a criminal gang. They commit crimes. Kingston was her enforcer. She hurts people."

I knew we were going to have this fight eventually, but I hated that it came just after we finally found the person we needed to stop. And just after I'd apologized about a previous fight. Shouting wouldn't work. We were too close together to make it anything other than a tantrum. I couldn't bully him into doing what I wanted; persuasion was my best approach. And that was easier if I looked like I was agreeing.

"Okay, Vince is probably our best way to go. He wants Joan cleared and he knows the world. Maybe even knows who's feeding the cops information. How do you know he will work with us?"

"I don't. There's a possibility no one will talk to us. Even if he won't help, he might give away something that leads us to the next person."

"And Kingston's friends?"

"You heard them. Only two of them might be connected through crime. Inga Sutton, his girlfriend, and Sherry Waters, arms dealer. Did you talk to either of them?"

I'd been pulled away from it after I spoke to Joe Turner. Val called, and then the threat, and then the opportunity to investigate cops. "No. Should we reach out first?"

Paul rubbed his eyes and sighed. "I forget you aren't a cop."

"Is that supposed to be a compliment?"

"Yes. But when I do that, I make mistakes. A cop would have logged the interviews and kept going until all the interviews were complete. The team would balance jobs so nothing slipped through the cracks."

And if I was working alone, I wouldn't have followed up because I wouldn't have access to police records. "Don't blame yourself, I dropped the ball. Do we go on with Vince, or stop and try to talk to the two women?"

He checked the screen before answering. "We go on with Vince. I have to believe that between Walker, Bracken, and Valette, one of them didn't want to kill a fellow cop. One of them got pushed too far. Vince is our best bet to get someone to turn."

Fight avoided. I was proud of my self-restraint. "So, we didn't screw up our case by missing Inga and Sherry. We can circle back if Vince doesn't agree. What's the new data?" I nodded toward the screen.

"Vince's arrest record. It's pretty thin. Either he's smarter than he likes to show, or Joan protected him. She needs someone around all the time. So the latter is probably right."

"Is there anything we can use as leverage?" Vince might agree if we applied a little blackmail. I didn't like to think of it that way, but blackmail was the right term.

"Maybe. Grab your notebook."

It only took ten minutes to go through the links. Vince's crimes were petty. They were all old, and none of our suspects had any connection. We could only hope he was in an accommodating mood.

"Call him and set up a meeting," Paul said. "He's more likely to agree if you invite him as Joan's detective."

I sent a text instead. If he balked, I'd follow up with a call. He responded within seconds. In two hours, in a coffee shop on The Drive, we'd have our answers.

"Before we head out, I want to make something clear." If I didn't speak now, events would sweep us along and I'd have no chance to put my case first.

Paul logged out of the database and shut down his laptop. "Okay, I'm listening."

"I want to stop this gang of cops. I think they will do more damage than Joan's whole gang if we let them go on."

"But? I can hear it's there, Charity."

"But my case is to prove Joan was framed. That's all. Rance was very clear about that. If it comes down to a choice, I will put my case first and be there to help you after I'm finished."

"Yeah. I know. I appreciate you bringing it up. I want her freed if she's innocent, but my priority is the corruption. I truly believe the two cases are so closely tied we won't run into a problem. But if we do, promise you won't just disappear. I can't be distracted from my case to make sure you're safe."

I wasn't as optimistic as he was that we wouldn't collide at some point. "I agree, and the same goes for you. If you disappear on me, I can't make an arrest. So no surprises, no lies."

He laughed and held out his hand to shake on the deal. "Okay. It's worth a try."

We shook hands and headed out to talk to Vince. On the way I tried to think if I was still holding on to any secrets that Paul should know.

I f you didn't already know the coffee shop was a hangout for criminals, you probably wouldn't be surprised. Not that every place that seemed populated with old men sipping espresso and watching soccer was a mob hangout, but the absence of women and anyone under seventy kind of sent that message.

Paul walked behind me as we went through the door. Maybe to signal we weren't a threat. The barista looked up and tilted his head toward a doorway at the back of the room. No offer of an espresso or a pastry.

The back room was darker than the front. No TV screens to enhance the glow from the low lighting. Only three round cafe tables stood in the space. Vince sat at the farthest one facing the entrance, and a thug sat at each of the other tables, pretending not to watch us.

I sat across from Vince. Paul took the chair beside me and moved it closer to Vince before sitting. A little power play. I hoped it wouldn't put Vince on the offensive. We needed him to feel cooperative.

"How long before Joan is out?" Vince asked.

"Working on it," I said. "We have a plan and need your help."

"Okay. I'm not promising, but go ahead, tell me."

I glanced at the thugs. They might not like hearing our idea. And Vince might not want to agree with them in the room. "Probably best if we're alone."

He looked at Paul and then at me. "He goes too."

"I'm not leaving Charity here alone," Paul said.

"She's not in danger. I'm not sending my guys out and sitting with a cop. You can see how that might look, right?"

"I'm fine. You can wait right outside."

Maybe it was naivety, but I didn't think Vince would do anything to me that risked screwing up Joan's case. Even if he'd decided to take over, too many people knew I was working for Rance. And he probably didn't want to piss off a great lawyer who seemed willing to defend his kind of crook.

Paul glared at me for a second as if he was trying to send me a message. Unfortunately, I didn't read scowl. He got up and waited for the thugs to do the same, then followed them out.

"What's the plan?" Vince asked. "Something you don't want my people to hear about ever, or just not until you've convinced me?"

He wasn't stupid. What I was about to ask could backfire, and Joan wasn't here to protect Vince if the cops went after him. "We need to set up a sting, but I have to be sure of a few things first."

He nodded for me to continue.

"I need to know if some specific cops are on your payroll, or if you know they're on someone's."

"You have names? That's a big step. Why do I think that's not what you really want to know?"

I gave him the names. He denied paying them for favors, and said he had no idea if they were working for someone else.

"Ask your next question," he said. "I promise you can walk out of here if you offend me. I'm not the Godfather, Charity. I can forgive you a lot because you're trying to get Joan out of jail."

"Are you or any of your gang members on someone's payroll?"

He barked out a laugh. "It doesn't work that way, Charity."

I didn't believe him. "What about another gang. Like Jackie Tomasino's?"

"I told you it doesn't work that way. No cop can force a guy like me to do anything. If we exchange favors, it's a business deal. Yes, we do that, but no one is working for a cop. There's no reason to. We're criminals; what can they hold over us?"

"Fine. I don't really care about favors. I want to set up the sting to catch a crooked cop. I need you to set it up."

"What you mean is you need me to sacrifice someone. I won't. Trust is the only thing that binds us as an organization. I start tossing my people to the cops, I wake up dead in an alley."

"It doesn't have to be a sacrifice. I want to catch a cop, and that means they don't get to arrest anyone."

"Only if it goes right. What if you're mistaken about this cop?"

Neither Paul nor I were questioning our assumptions. I couldn't give Vince the facts because I would be arming him with blackmail fodder. He wouldn't believe me if I said he should trust me.

"I've done this before," I said. "Set a trap with a gang leader. It worked, and his people didn't retaliate."

"I know who you mean," Vince said. "Our organization doesn't work by the same rules."

If I couldn't find a way to change his mind, we'd be back at square one — well, okay, square ten, but it was still a step backward.

"What if Joan said it was okay?"

"She won't. Believe me, Charity. This isn't going to fly. Jackie won't do it either, just in case you were thinking of asking him. We need the cops we pay for, and they're corrupt. I get that your targets are worse, but corruption is corruption. We turn on one group, we lose all our assets."

"I gave you those names," I said. "What will happen to them?" If he went to recruit them, maybe Paul and I could work the trap without his cooperation. It didn't matter to me if he was a willing participant or not.

"Let's say I know them. We don't work with them, and I'm pretty sure they don't work with anyone on our side of the law, but I could be wrong. I'll pretend I never heard their names, so you have a clear run at them."

"Why should I believe you?"

"Good question. Think about it. If you're right, that group of cops isn't stopping at blackmail or taking bribes for releasing criminals — or framing one. Why would they need to align with us? They have too much power. I hope you're successful, but I can't risk my people, and Joan wouldn't thank me for doing it."

46

W e should have made a backup plan. I was convinced that the plan would work because of my case with the Hells Angels. I guess crooked cops were more of a threat than a deranged Russian mob boss.

"What now?" I asked Paul as we walked back to the car. "Do we try Jackie?"

"No. I have another idea." He unlocked the doors of the car and waited until I strapped in. "Tomasino is going to say the same thing, Vince was right about that. We need a weaker link. Someone who might want a way out of jail. Someone who will do anything for a deal. And we don't need a go-between."

So back to the start? Whether we were right about Evelyn or not, someone was leading a gang of crooked cops. And they knew we were close, if the increase of the threat level was any indication. I was the only one being threatened, as far as I knew. If Paul knew differently and kept it to himself, I wouldn't know until it was too late. "Like they're doing to me? I'm the weak link here, right? A civilian with no way of proving I'm innocent of any charges they make?"

"Not so much," Paul said. "You have friends in the department. You did good work on the Hargreaves case. The RCMP are going to stand behind you. And I wouldn't get any threats. If this goes deep enough, one day Professional Standards will just call me in for a talk."

Maybe the threats were better. At least I had a heads up. "How do they know we're close? I thought you were being careful."

"I am, but the databases log all access attempts. If they look at my code, they can make the same conclusions as we do. And I don't think any corrupt cop would think twice about violating my privacy. Unless you've been telling someone the details of our investigation, we don't have a leak. It's only you and me, Charity."

I didn't answer. If someone was talking, it had to be Paul. But he was right. Knowing our activity was traceable was completely different from knowing someone was tracing us. "What's your idea?"

He pulled into the Bayshore parking lot and found an empty spot. "Let's get coffee. If I'm right, we won't be stopping much tonight.

I followed him to the coffee shop. Three people sat on stools at the counter. We took a table in the far corner and Paul got us coffee and pastries.

"Tell me if this sounds like a good idea," he said. "We go back to your place and check some more records."

"But we've spent hours doing that already. Sounds like we'll just be spinning wheels." I didn't mean to sound like a sulky teenager, but it came out exactly that way.

"Let me finish. We've been looking into the records of the police involved. There are civilian employees."

"And we'll find all kinds of activity in a database for people who aren't cops?" A civilian would be our weak link for certain.

"It's more complicated. They don't sign off on official documents, but there's a log of activities assigned to civilians. What we need will be there. Some connection to Johnson or Moore. Something that at least proves to us which of them is involved."

I was sure our culprit was Evelyn. Why would she forge Ted's signature if it wasn't to use his authority? I guess Paul needed something more than that to take her down.

Now that I think of it, she could have just been saving time, or Ted might have told her to go ahead and sign his name. I hated not knowing. The only thing that saved me from kicking a wall was the sure knowledge that one piece of clear evidence was all we needed to get Joan free. Then we'd be able to take our time to build a corruption case.

"So we find our bit of real proof, and then we go after whoever ordered Zoe's death and set Joan up?"

He ate the last of his chocolate croissant and brushed the crumbs off his lap. "Probably a few more steps involved, but yeah, that's the idea."

47

K nowing what we were looking for made the search easy. Within ten minutes, Paul had identified two civilian employees who were up to something. That could be unrelated, but we needed more actual files to determine if it was pertinent to our case. He went to the station to pull the files and I ordered dinner.

While I waited, I pulled down all the notes from the wall, sorted out the ones that turned out to be unrelated, and then grouped the remainder by individual. I added notes about what we'd found, and when I was finished, Evelyn's role was clear. Ted's cluster had five notes. The three uniformed officers each had under fifteen. Evelyn had thirty.

It wasn't proof yet, but it was damning and gave us a focus. If we had someone to turn, cop or civilian, this data was all ammunition.

The security gate buzzed for admittance; the delivery guy from the Thai restaurant. I let him through the gate and stepped outside my door to watch him walk the finger dock.

Paul grabbed the gate before it latched and came behind. We were ready.

We filled bowls with dinner and left the remainder on the kitchen counter. The files we laid out on the coffee table. Personnel files for Bill, Chris, and Lucy, and our two civilians, Kyle Timmins and Hope Greenisle.

"Moore and Johnson's files are missing," Paul said.

"Suspicious." I pointed out the newly organized wall notes. "She's our leader, right?"

"Yes. Professional Standards will get the file if we can give them something that points to her. We'll have enough soon."

That easy mention of Professional Standards was weird. Most cops I knew didn't exactly hate them, but there was usually a bit of a negative vibe. Kind of like how most people felt about the dentist. You need them to keep you healthy, but who really liked to go to them? Paul talked like he respected the Professional Standards officers.

"I should probably be the one to go to Professional Standards, right? If you do it, you'll face retribution from your fellow officers?"

"Maybe, but if anyone wants to make a big deal of it, they'll come after you too."

"I'm used to a certain level of irritation from the force," I said. "It comes with the territory."

He laughed as he flipped open Kyle's folder. "We'll see."

Kyle's personnel file didn't reveal much. But there were a few notes about attitude, and Paul noticed a link between his work days and computer problems. "I'll flag him for his boss, but I don't see him as part of a criminal conspiracy," Paul said as he flipped the file closed.

Hope Greenisle's information was clean too. It didn't mesh with the hints we'd found in the database, which bugged me. I flipped back to the hiring paperwork. "How deep a check does the VPD do for civilian employees?"

"Same as any other organization, why?"

I took a picture of her ID with my phone and started an image search. "This seems like too big a gap between what we found and what's here. Okay, I was right." I turned my phone so he could see the result of the search. Hope Greenisle was really a journalist named Lisa Howell.

"Great," Paul said, opening his email. "I'll report her now, so she'll be gone by the morning. We don't need her researching the force at all, but if she gets wind of our investigation, we'll never solve it."

I guess that was some kind of result. Two people who shouldn't be working for the VPD would be gone. It didn't help us at all with our case. "Wasted time, then."

"Eliminating a lead is progress." He opened the three police files, laying them out on the coffee table so we could review them together. "Back to our plan to catch one of these."

Without someone to set a trap, this was going to be hard. "How did you get these files?"

"Don't worry, no one saw me. But I have to get them back in a couple of hours so they won't be missed."

"Why did you say you couldn't get them earlier?"

He looked up from Bill's file, placing his finger on the page to keep his place. "You think I lied? Why would I do that? I want this case closed as much as you do. Maybe more than you."

"Not an answer."

His eyes tightened at the corners. I'd poked at one of his buttons. He didn't like having to justify his actions. Or I'd caught him in a big fat lie.

"Okay. I didn't think at the time it was worth the risk. We

didn't have enough to justify taking the files if I got caught. I should have said that up front."

"Are you holding back anything else?"

"Not that I can think of, Charity. Look, you don't know the system, so you have no idea what I'm balancing when I take information or give you access to records. It will all be forgiven if we prove our case, but we've been fishing for direction up to now. If someone caught me, I'd be suspended, and you would be on your own. And worse, Moore would be warned."

It felt like I had a choice. I could believe him and get on with the investigation, or I could give in to my paranoia about cops and work alone. I had enough right now for Rance to get Joan cleared. Not proof for court, but enough to convince the Crown that the case would be full of doubt. That wasn't enough for me. If I walked away now, I'd carry guilt about letting Evelyn run her little gang. They killed Kingston and Zoe, and I couldn't leave that hanging. And I was really tired of feeling stuck between the two choices of trust or distrust.

"Fine. Let's get these assholes."

48

I f I'd thought about it with even a little focus, I would have realized the database only contained summaries. Who was going to sit and enter every detail from a paper file into a computer? Or, more accurately, who would pay for that kind of diligence? Each of the files on the coffee table contained pages of incidents.

"Why isn't any of this noted online?" Surely if there was a trend of bad or questionable behavior, there was a place to keep track of it.

"Because nothing was followed through on. The database is too easily accessed to keep complaints that turned out to be baseless. No one gets access to these files unless they have the authority, or a court order."

Or were able to sneak in after hours? I didn't say it because we'd closed that topic and I wasn't willing to take any time to dig it up again.

"Yes, but look at Bill's, for example." I laid out the sheets across the files. "Ten recent complaints about excessive force. All signed off by Evelyn. All dismissed, eight of them based on the testimony of Lucy or Chris. Isn't that a trend?"

"Yes, for us. If we weren't looking for similarities, it wouldn't be so obvious. They partner on and off. Your partner is your backup — for good or bad."

"He harassed Kingston four times."

Paul separated those reports out. "It's weird that Kingston complained about it. Getting hassled by cops is part of the job for a criminal. Someone told him to call us. Joan?"

"Sending a message that she wasn't going to let the cops push her around?" It would explain why they set her up. "Or that's why he was killed? By Joan or someone else trying to shut him up?"

"Possibly. Hard to prove." He tucked all the papers into Bill's folder. "It's pretty much the same for Valette and Bracken. Some hassling complaints, one excessive force on Valette. All signed off by Moore. But this is interesting." He passed me a signed statement from Lucy's file and then looked through Chris's.

It was a statement signed by Lucy and mentioning Chris. A case of petty theft, which was thrown out on a technicality. The accused wasn't named, just a file number. "Why would this be in the personnel file?"

"Someone thought it might be fishy. There's a copy in Bracken's file. I'll check the case files to see if there are any other notes."

He pulled out his laptop. I waited while he searched, trying to think through the possibilities. It could be legitimate, or they were ordered to blow the case for a reason.

"Kid named Wallace Danes. Shoplifting. Multiple cases all thrown out."

"That's why it's fishy? Because someone keeps screwing up and he gets away with it?"

"Six dismissals. Four of them touch on Walker, Bracken,

and Valette. Yeah. That's a flag. But unless there's some reason to follow up, no one will take the time. It's shoplifting, not murder."

I thought of arguing that not facing the consequences of petty crime is why criminals went on to more serious offenses, but decided to keep quiet. Paul knew that was true. And the cops were spread thin enough. I pulled out my phone and did a search on the name. "Got him on Instagram. Smart-assed idiot. Posts how he gets away with whatever he does because he's got connections."

"Well, kids are stupid," Paul said. "Does he say who he's connected to?"

I did a deeper search, and the answer was right in front of me. "He's Evelyn Moore's nephew. You think we should talk to him?"

"No. He's an idiot and won't have any details. And he'll go running to Moore as soon as we reach out."

"She's getting him off charges, which must be against the rules. Is that enough to get her taken in?" I would prefer to catch her myself, but if we reported her, she'd be stopped for a while. And maybe an investigation into her actions would lead to the corruption.

"It's against the rules, but it happens enough that her union rep will shut down any investigation. We can use it to get more, though. And it's leverage against her three minions."

"If we can't use the information we find, what are we doing with it?"

"Building our case, Charity. We need to present solid proof of wrongdoing before we report her. If we show the evidence against Walker, Bracken, and Valette to Professional Standards, they'll take action on those three and we'll lose our leverage. It won't take long for Moore to replace them."

"Then we turn one of them, like we planned."

"Yes. But we don't have enough yet. I figure the easiest to turn will be Walker. He was watching you for a reason. It could be he thinks Moore will turn on him."

I didn't know if I agreed with Paul. I mean, yes, Bill was watching me when we found him in the coffee shop, but he could have been there on Evelyn's orders. "Why do you think he was doing it for himself rather than Evelyn?"

"She's the one threatening you. Surveillance is too subtle for her. If she sent him, then she would have made sure you found out."

"We don't know that the calls are coming from Evelyn."

"Do you think it's someone else?"

"No, but it could be. Okay. Say I agree with you about Bill. How do we get to him?"

Paul checked the time. "I have to take these files back in a few minutes. Is there anything else we can pull before I do?"

I longed for one of those personality tests. One that told us Bill's weakness so we could hit it hard. But if the VPD did them, the records were kept somewhere else. "No. Take them back and then we make a plan to trap Bill."

49

There was no point in just sitting and wishing that Paul didn't have to keep running back to base so we wouldn't get caught with files. My living room was starting to look like a bomb had exploded in it, so I let my brain work on a trap while I tidied up all the papers we'd scattered around. Unfortunately, that took only five minutes, and Paul wouldn't be back for another half hour even with the lack of traffic at this time of night.

My phone rang just as I was about to start scribbling ideas for a sting.

Jackie Tomasino. Interesting.

"What do you want?" I wasn't going to dance around politely for this guy.

"I'm out," he said. "That shit charge didn't stick. You called the cops on me, right?"

Oh great, another person with a grudge against me based on no facts. "No. Did you call just to threaten me? If so, take a number."

"Just wanted to eliminate you from my list. Someone

called in a tip just after we met. You can't blame me for thinking the worst."

"I'm busy."

"I got a tip for you. Something that helps Joan. I want her to know it was me, right?"

"So she owes you a favor." I didn't much like facilitating a relationship between two crime bosses, but what happened after this case was closed was none of my business — unless they dragged me into whatever came from it.

"Or we're even, you don't need to keep the tally," he said. "Look, you want to close your case, but I'm guessing it's not going anywhere."

No need for him to know about our progress. "The tip?"

"Look into the cops involved. You'll get your answers if you ask the right questions."

So no real help. "Which cops? What questions?"

"You want me to do your whole job?"

I didn't have anything much to do until Paul got back, so keeping Jackie talking would fill some time. "No, but I don't see Joan being grateful to you for a tip that consists of 'look at some unnamed cops'. Is that all you have?"

"Maybe I'm just testing you. See if you're smart enough. Okay, I was arrested by this cop called Bill Walker. It was a shit charge. Someone wanted me off the streets for a few days."

How would that help anything? If Jackie was a problem for Evelyn, then why not set him up for a real crime? There must be plenty. "Why would sticking you in custody help anything?"

"If I knew that, I'd tell you. Here's the thing. He took a call in the car. Someone telling him to make sure I couldn't get in the way. I only heard his side of the conversation, but he has a habit of repeating what someone says. Scared to get it wrong, maybe."

Jackie had been in jail for just over two days. Zoe's murder was the only event that came to mind during that time, and I couldn't imagine Jackie getting in the middle of that. "How do we know what happened while you were inside?"

"Could be anything. I got the idea this cop didn't know either, and the other person didn't say it for him to repeat."

It was information and about the cop we were about to trap into turning on the boss. "Is that it?"

"You got somewhere to be?"

"Yes."

"This Walker guy is scared." His voice was hard, and the words snapped out. He didn't like to be pushed. "I'm telling you something bad happened and he was not happy about it. Maybe they just wanted to use my neighborhood to do something. Maybe they thought I was competing on a deal somewhere. I don't know how a crooked cop thinks beyond the usual greed and entitlement."

"What is your neighborhood?"

"Did something happen around Clark Drive, maybe the north end?"

He wasn't going to tell me where he operated, but that was enough. "Are you saying you don't know? I find that hard to believe."

"Maybe I heard about it from some inside sources. Someone is going to take the fall for it, and I'll do anything I need to so it's not me."

Zoe's murder took on a new significance. Why hadn't I thought they'd look for a scapegoat? It wouldn't be Jackie, at least; too many complications to prove he ordered the hit from jail. Anyone else involved was fair game. Vince, or

Jackie's second in command. Any of the enforcers they used. Any criminal Evelyn wanted off the streets.

Paul.

Me.

"Okay. I'll let Joan know you helped."

"You owe me, too," he said. "I don't pass on information for free."

Jerk. "This is only worth one favor. You want it from me, or from a criminal competitor?"

"You might help with the cops," he said.

He had no idea how little leverage I had with my cop friends. Mostly because I would never ask anyone to break the law for me. "Nope."

"Fine." He ended the call.

50

Paul arrived back at my place ten minutes later. Long enough for me to sort through the implications of what Jackie told me. The fact that he'd called me for this favor was suspicious. I had no idea how reliable his facts were. It could all be a ruse. If I accused a cop of corruption, and he proved he wasn't corrupt, I'd get labeled by the cops as someone not to be trusted. That would affect my relationship with the cops, and David's by association — and Leigh's.

But what would Jackie gain out of that? There were easier ways of keeping his competitor off the streets, including having someone stick a shiv in her while she was locked up. If he had the facts wrong, he didn't know. So either we had the truth, and confirmation that Bill was our best bet to turn on Evelyn, or someone was using Jackie.

I told Paul everything as soon as he sat down on my sofa.

"I can verify some of it," he said. "We can see who brought Jackie in, but even if it's Walker, do you want to just accuse him? We were going to trap him anyway, and he sounds like a better option now we know he was scared."

"I think we stick with our plan unless there's no other option. I feel like we're on the brink of solving this whole mess. Jackie's call is a sidetrack we don't need to explore."

"And you won't be doing a criminal favors," Paul said.

True. The problem we faced was a lack of plan. Before I could say anything, someone knocked.

We both froze and stared at the door.

"You expecting visitors? At three in the morning?"

It had to be one of my neighbors. Delores and Justin? If it was them, then Delores would be complaining about something. The tenant at Jake's place? I hadn't seen her for a few days. My other three neighbors were like ghosts, rarely seen and never socialized with.

"No. Stay here. I'll close the door enough to hide you." I didn't wait for him to agree.

"Who is it?" I asked when I got to the door.

"Open up," a woman said.

Whoever it was stood to the side so I couldn't see her through the peephole. I relied on the security gate to keep strangers out of the neighborhood, so I'd never installed a door camera. I regretted that now. "Who are you?"

"Someone you don't want hanging out on your dock."

I didn't recognize the voice. I ran through the women we had on our list. Evelyn was unlikely to come here to confront me; she'd send someone. So this could be Lucy Valette. Or it could be Kingston's old girlfriend, Inga, or Sherry, his arms dealer friend. Or someone completely off my radar. I glanced back at Paul. He was watching from the living room, his weapon ready. I waved him to the side so he'd stay hidden.

I'd have to open the door, and unless this woman intended to shoot me as soon as I gave her a target, I was safe enough.

I unlocked the deadbolt and yanked the door, moving to the side just in case.

A blond woman in her mid-thirties stepped into view.

"How did you get through the gate?"

"Followed a drunk neighbor."

She made a move to enter my home. I blocked her way, keeping her just on the other side of the doorway. "Who are you?" I recognized her from the station hassling, but I didn't want her to know she'd made any impact.

"I'm surprised you don't know already. I guess you're not as good as your reputation."

"You're a cop?" I didn't wait for her to respond. "Lucy Valette?"

"I have some information for you. Are you going to invite me in, or do you want your nosy next door neighbor to hear everything?"

I leaned around to check Delores' home. Sure enough, a light shone from the kitchen. To give her credit, Delores wasn't just nosy, she protected our little neighborhood. And she'd taken care of me more than once. I didn't want to put anyone in danger, so I stepped aside.

She looked around my kitchen area like she was thinking of buying the place. I pointed her to a chair and sat beside her. "Start talking."

"It would help if you told me where you are in the investigation. I don't want to repeat anything and waste your time."

"Let me worry about my time. If you don't tell me what you came for, I'll call the cops and lodge a complaint about harassment."

"Really? Harassment? I just came and knocked on your door."

"At three am. And through a security gate, without buzzing for entry."

I wasn't going to complain because it would slow down our investigation, but she didn't know that. And whoever sent her probably didn't want any scrutiny that Paul could turn into a full-blown corruption investigation.

"Do you know where Detective Grewal is right now?"

"Why?"

"He's not a good guy. He has a past; you can't rely on him."

Jeez, did she think I was stupid? Probably still fishing. "I don't know where he is. I generally don't keep track of people I barely know."

"Isn't he working with you?"

"Why would he?"

"Just a rumor."

"It's time you left," I said. "I'm not going to give you any information, and you just came here to find out how close I am to getting Joan Tiller out of jail."

"No. Look, someone is killing people, and they're not going to stop until they feel safe. You need to back off."

"I'm only concerned with the death of Kingston Dupre. Someone killed him and framed Joan Tiller. My job is to find proof. I don't know about any other murders."

"There have been more. I'm not going to tell you who if you don't know already. You can't trust the people you've talked to."

"How do you know who I'm talking to?" Had she just slipped up and let me know I was under surveillance?

"I don't know, but I can make an assumption. Vince Carmichael? Jackie Tomasino?"

I didn't react to either name.

"They had every reason to set her up. It's going to be a gang problem, you know that."

I stood and gestured for her to join me. "I want you to go. You clearly don't have anything to add to my investigation other than pointing fingers at suspects and vaguely threatening me. If you were good at your job, you'd know the most obvious answer is usually wrong."

This time she didn't argue about leaving. I held the door for her and she stepped out to the finger dock. "You are going to regret taking this case if you continue."

I didn't say anything. She marched toward the gate, and I watched until she was through before I stepped back inside. If I thought for a second that we could turn her, I'd call her back. She wasn't scared at all. She was happy to follow orders blindly. We'd have no leverage on her.

Paul slid the pocket door open and joined me.

"I texted David about our visitor."

"He's staying with a buddy until this is over," I said. "I don't want him to come home just because we got threatened."

"He's not coming. But you can't keep this stuff from him, Charity. He trusts you for some reason, don't exploit that."

51

"I didn't think it at the time," I said. "But maybe we've picked the wrong cop to turn. Could Lucy be covering up fear? I mean, she didn't really do anything while she was here."

"You could be right," Paul said. "But she might have come on orders to intimidate us. She also might have come just to find out how confident you were, and the threat was tossed in on the off chance you'd stop."

If everything could be interpreted so many ways, we'd never take the next step forward. I decided to stop second-guessing myself and get on with hunting our suspect. "Okay, I guess we just have to pick an answer and hope we get it right?"

"Charity, I wasn't throwing up roadblocks," he said. "Don't deny it. I can read your face like a book. We can't change our target with every reaction. We thought Walker was our guy. Valette's visit doesn't change that. He was nervous enough to stalk you. Jackie told us he was afraid on the phone."

"Okay, but she might be watching us and reporting back.

We can't set a trap if we're being observed. We might get Bill killed before we talk to him. And how did she know we were close, anyway?"

My mind was hopping all over the place. Probably the lack of sleep and the stress reaction to being threatened in my home. But I couldn't just get back on track without talking about what she'd done.

"Remember, every search we made was logged," Paul said. "If I was running this gang and I knew someone was looking into a frame-up I ordered, I'd be watching for traces of the investigation. We searched a lot of stuff that didn't result in a lead for the case, so Moore isn't sure how far along we are. That's to our benefit right now, but it won't last long."

"I should go out and check to see if anyone is watching." A quick survey of the area wouldn't take long and might help me focus. Living in the middle of a marina came with the advantage of seclusion. There were only so many places to hide surveillance.

"No. If anyone goes, it's me." He ran his hand under the table and then the chair. "She might have left a listening device."

"I could see her hands the whole time. And if she had, we've already said too many names to pretend we don't know who's in charge."

He gave a quick nod. "I should have thought about it earlier. Okay, we don't have much time; we need to set the trap and spring it now."

"How? If we're being watched, it won't work. If we tip our hand too early, then we get Walker killed. It's not like they're shy about getting rid of cops." It was starting to feel familiar. My last case was littered with dead bodies as the Russian mob boss we were trying to capture killed anyone who might be in his way.

"Moore is too smart to just kill one of her people. Smith wasn't part of her gang. It's different for Walker. Killing him sends a message to the other two, and she's going to be afraid it will turn them against her."

"Okay. So we need to make sure we're safe to act, then call Bill Walker to a meeting, and then spring the trap." It sounded so simple.

"I'll go check the area and text you if I see anything."

"Why wouldn't you just come back and tell me?"

"I want to find out where everyone is right now. Walker might be on shift, or on leave, or tucked up in bed after finishing a night shift."

"Or he's already been killed. If we know he's vulnerable, Evelyn will know it too."

"Yes. But like I said, killing him is a big risk. She'll probably try to talk to him first. I won't be gone long. This is going to be over by lunch time."

I hated agreeing with the plan. Some paranoid little voice in my head was telling me I was being sidelined. "How long? I'm not waiting for hours only to find out you finished up the case behind my back."

"A couple of hours at most." He didn't look at me when he said the words.

"Okay. Go before she disappears." He picked up his bag and reached to close his laptop and pack it.

"No. If you're coming back that fast, you don't need to take your stuff."

He stared at me for a second before dropping the bag back on the floor. "Fine. What are you planning on doing while I'm gone? I don't want you rushing off to solve the case without me either."

I laughed. "You'd think we don't trust each other. I promise I won't go poking at anyone to make them react. I'll write up my report for Rance. I'll get breakfast if I can find a place open this early. I'll call David and tell him we're almost done so he can come home."

"Okay. I'll call you if anything changes."

I watched him walk down the finger dock to the security gate. If we were being observed, then Lucy would know Paul was hiding within earshot while she was trying to intimidate me. Nothing we could do about that any more than we could have fixed the problem if we'd found a bug. It felt like we were committed now. Just a few facts to get us on the way. One trap. One confession. And then we'd go back to our regular lives. Boring insurance cases were looking good right now.

52

A s soon as the gate shut behind Paul, I dashed inside. His laptop sat open on the coffee table. He'd forgotten to log out from our last session. Poking around in his databases wasn't breaking my promise. Databases weren't people. I didn't care that he'd see it differently; I had the chance to do one more poke and I didn't want to let it go to waste. Maybe I could find that one last link with Evelyn that let me finish my case, and allowed the cops to take her off the streets.

Springing a trap on Bill was still our best plan with what we knew. If it worked, the case would be over for me. But not for Evelyn. I wanted her in prison for what she'd done. Criminals were bad enough, but a corrupt cop could do so much more damage. And Bill might be the only one to take the fall if we didn't have real evidence that pointed to her.

If that was the outcome of our plan, then I'd be in more danger from the rest of the gang.

I started at the beginning of the searches. A menu of all the different sources available. Not all of them would help with someone of Evelyn's rank. But I wondered when she started her little empire. Was she recruited by anyone, or did she simply build from scratch? I hoped for the second, because otherwise we'd need to find out who she took over from.

I started with a folder labeled 'Open Cases'. Checking if our four suspects were linked to any cases that were still active might give me an idea who they were leveraging now. A case in limbo was perfect fodder for extortion. A threat to tip the investigation with false evidence if not paid to tip it the other way.

Ten cases popped up on the screen. Each person was arrested by one of our three beat cops and the charge signed off by Evelyn. Were they getting sloppy? Up to now, we'd had to dig quite hard to find links between them. Now ten cases all tied together? I made note of the details and then checked the time. Fifteen minutes since Paul left, and he hadn't texted that I was being watched. I guess that meant I wasn't.

I looked at the people arrested in all cases. Eight had links to Joan's organization. The other two were on outstanding warrants from Alberta and Prince Edward Island. I discounted them as legitimate. So it looked to me like Evelyn was targeting Joan's people. Why hadn't Vince noticed? Or had he noticed, but didn't want to tell me? Was Vince compromised? Did I want Joan to ask that question? Probably not.

I went back to the beginning again. There was a folder labeled 'Shift Schedule'. I checked the date and time of Zoe's death. Only Bill was on shift, but I remembered from the report that Chris had reported on the crash.

I looked at my notes and then scanned the walls. Paul was right; I had enough to close my case with Rance. Nothing concrete about who actually framed Joan, but enough to raise significant doubt about her guilt. He'd be able to get her out of jail, at least. I picked up a highlighter and marked every note that would help clear Joan.

From my research in the last twenty minutes, it was apparent that Chris, Bill, and Lucy took orders. Nothing pointed to them instigating anything. Bill might be the weak link, but he might not have what we needed to take down Evelyn. We needed to go after her.

I returned to the menu and did a broad search on just her name, no rank, because I wanted everything.

The results started to fill the screen and kept going for a few minutes. I tried not to read anything into the number of links; she'd been a cop for a long time.

When the final link showed up, I scrolled through the whole list. It looked like the returns were in chronological order, which helped. I started at the bottom, the oldest, and made notes.

In a half hour I'd found the point where she turned. For her first five years as a sergeant, she appeared to be a good cop. She'd made the rank pretty young. Then a few complaints showed up. Sloppy work, mostly. A little insub-ordination. A short medical leave — six weeks. Possibly rehab, or punishment for falsely reporting corruption. Then her file was clean. Too clean. Like she'd spent more time keeping her image professional than actually being a cop. Not great.

As I got closer to the current activity, I noted her signa-ture on more cases involving organized crime. She'd signed a few reports on Kuznetsov's gang, but none of them went to trial. Of the twenty she signed for, sixteen had charges dropped and two had been killed in prison. The other two were fugitives. Probably back in Russia. No one had noticed the pattern, and I guess I did her a favor by getting

Kuznetsov charged, because she'd likely have been on his kill list.

I had enough to start an investigation on her. I needed Paul to report everything to Professional Standards. I considered logging out of the database, but decided to leave that until I reached Paul. I picked up my phone and saw text notifications. I flipped it to the side; the silent mode button was showing red again. I flipped it back and read the texts, all from Paul.

No one watching unless from an apartment.

Then a few minutes later, *I'll be back in an hour.*

I checked the time. Still fifteen minutes to go.

Then all caps.

GET OUT OF MY LAPTOP. SHE'S ON SHIFT AND LOOKING AT ALERTS!!!!!!!

53

I slapped the lid down on the laptop and reeled back in my seat. I didn't know what good it would do; maybe stop her tracking the location? Had Paul guessed I'd been digging into the data, or had he left it open on purpose, knowing I wouldn't be able to resist?

Why did Evelyn think to look for someone investigating her? *Did* Paul mean Evelyn when he said 'she'? Too many questions that I had no idea how to answer.

For a second, I considered tossing the laptop into the marina; but if it *was* Evelyn, she knew where I was, and if she had us under surveillance despite Paul's assurances, she knew I was alone.

Fine, I needed information. I sent a text to Paul asking for more details and when he'd be back. He didn't respond immediately. I was going to have to deal with this myself. I snatched all the notes off the wall. If I was about to be invaded, I could try to save our work for Paul or David to find after they dealt with my dead body.

The notes went into a folder and then I jammed it between two others in the hidden cabinet. The way the sliding doors were built, they were invisible unless you knew where to look. The laptop was a different matter. If it could be tracked, I didn't want someone breaking my walls to find everything.

The damage was already done anyway. If Evelyn started tracking who'd been looking at her files, it would take about two-point-four seconds to pinpoint the access. Paul! The access was his, not mine. Did that mean I was safe?

No. Lucy found me or was sent to my place.

Paul still hadn't responded. It had only been a couple of minutes, although my adrenaline-flooded brain thought I'd been dithering for hours.

Time to get out into a public space where I'd be harder to trap.

My phone rang as I was pulling on my jacket.

Unknown number.

If I ignored it, I could go, but maybe Paul was using someone else's phone. I couldn't afford to risk it.

As soon as I connected, a woman spoke.

"You shouldn't poke around in official business."

Nothing disguising her voice this time. A bit husky, like she was recovering from a chest cold. It had to be Evelyn.

I didn't speak.

"Scaring you off didn't work, so let's talk."

I looked for the little red light that showed an active recording. "Go ahead."

"Not on the phone, and not now. Later."

So she could set me up? "Now, or I take what I have to Professional Standards."

"You think you have enough?"

"Yes." I had enough to get their attention, and Paul could convince someone to dig deeper.

"Then we don't need to meet."

"What are you going to add to my investigation?" Hopefully a recorded confession and all the dirt on her little gang.

"Everything. And everyone."

We must've been close to catching her if she was ready to turn on the whole operation. I'd bet good money the truth would be buried in a steaming pile of lies. "So what are you waiting for? I can't give you a deal, but I'm happy to listen."

"Not on the phone. Too many people could be listening."

I could argue with her, but it wasn't going to change Evelyn's mind. It was only around six pm and there were plenty of public places. I'd call Paul and at least give him our location.

"Where?"

"You know Woodland Park on McLean?"

A small community park near where Zoe died. It was bordered on two sides with houses, one side with apartments, and the final side with small industrial businesses. Not exactly out in the open, but not isolated either. "I know it."

"I'll be waiting for you in front of the crow mural. Get there fast." The call ended.

Look, I wasn't stupid. This could be a setup. Probably was one. But I couldn't miss the opportunity to trick her into telling me something. I'd have my phone on. I'd leave messages for Paul, David, and Leigh. I'd make sure I wasn't taken to a second location. And I'd change into my boots. I could run in them, and a kick did more damage when it was delivered with a steel toe.

I called Paul again and got his voicemail. I got David's and Leigh's as well. I guess it was too much to expect them to sit around waiting for me to call for help. I left detailed messages for all three about where I was going, what time

I'd be leaving home, where the notes and files were hidden, and for Paul, a confirmation that his laptop was sitting on the kitchen table, powered off.

For a brief second, I regretted never getting a gun permit. Then I was thankful. I'd probably end up shooting myself, or an innocent bystander. Evelyn would be armed. I just needed to be vigilant and fast.

And to hope my luck held for one more stupid act.

54

The meeting place was deserted. Part of me was happy that no innocent bystanders would be caught in the middle if things went wrong; the other, larger part worried that there would be no witnesses in the same circumstance.

The streetlights cast pools of illumination that didn't spread far into the park. I could make out the fence behind home plate on the baseball diamond, and a faint outline of the building near the community garden, but that was it. Evelyn could have an army of cops waiting to pounce from the shadows.

These thoughts were not helping me with my anxiety about coming here on my own. I'd already reached out to Paul, David, and Leigh again, but only got voicemail. I made one more attempt at contact by sending a group text. If I died, no one could say I hadn't asked for assistance.

I slid my phone into my pocket with the recording app running. With luck, she'd be on time and I'd get her confession for the case. That was, if the plan went better than the last time I'd left an open call to the RCMP while I faced down a kidnapper. Another story, but if I took my own advice, I wouldn't expect technology to work miracles.

Light shone across the mural of flying crows, a handful of butterflies, and a gardening moose. The building was for lease and locked up tight. Evelyn would have nowhere to hide inside if she ran.

I waited with my back against the wall, scanning the street to avoid being surprised. My car was a block away because there was no room to park closer. Evelyn would have the same problem unless she brought a patrol car and was willing to double-park.

A woman appeared around the corner and strode toward me as if she didn't want to chance me leaving. Evelyn.

"Let's go," she said. "My car is just behind the building. We can talk somewhere more comfortable."

Really? She thought I'd go to a second location? "Not going anywhere," I said. "Talk here, or in my car if you want more privacy."

"Smart. Okay. There's some stacked pallets in the parking lot, we can sit and talk in private, but not confined. That work?"

I looked at her. She was older than me but not by too much, maybe mid-forties. Medium height, medium build, medium brown hair tied back in a bun. If it came down to a fight, we'd probably be evenly matched. My added height and youth against her desperation. Well, not so even, but I'd have a chance. And maybe it would be harder for her to hide accomplices in an open lot. "Lead the way."

In seconds we were each perched on a stack of discarded pallets that must have belonged to one of the other businesses on the block. The parking lot was shared, so we might face interruption by a delivery. I was willing to risk it.

"Where's your sidekick?" she asked.

"Who?" We were here to talk about her crimes, not about the location of any cop.

"You know who I mean. Paul Grewal. The guy you set up by using his access to classified databases."

What was she, a spy? "You mean the guy I worked with to get you to stop? I have no idea. What did you come to say?"

She smiled like we were both in on a private joke. I didn't respond.

"What do you know so far?" she eventually asked. "I don't want to stall by hashing over details you already know."

It's like she was using the same script as Lucy had earlier. "It's not going to work that way. You tell me the story, or I go to Professional Standards with what I already have." This was starting to feel very much like a stupid idea.

She wiped her face with both hands and then put them in her lap. "I didn't mean to let everything go so far. I just wanted a little control. Not getting a chance at promotion made me invisible to everyone. So I decided to pick a few recruits before someone told them the dirty rumors. People I could count on to support me."

"So, you decided being a dirty cop was better than being a good one?"

That stiffened her body, and I watched as she got control. She unclenched her jaw and rubbed her palms on her thighs as she stared at the ground. If this was an act, she was overdoing it.

"I'm a good cop," she finally said, looking up at me. "I can't help it if other people made mistakes."

"So you set up your little gang," I said, prompting her to continue. I was in no mood to listen to her pitiful excuses.

"I just wanted someone to be on my side. But they, the recruits, all decided that we should get a bit of money for our troubles."

"So you threw cases for money?"

"Yes." She glared at me and squeezed her hands into fists. "Nothing big."

"What else? Or did you go from a little blackmail to murder overnight?"

"Zoe's death was Lucy's idea. You think I'm the leader? No, those three are blackmailing me into complying."

All lies, but I didn't want to slow down the story with accusations. "What about Kingston?"

"That thug? He deserved it."

"And Joan Tiller?"

"Bill said she stopped paying, so we needed to send a message."

None of her minions had the authority to get away with these crimes. If a patrol officer took any of the actions needed to commit the crimes she described, they would be reined in and probably fired, at minimum. "Why did you decide to talk to me?"

"You ask too many questions." She stood before I could react, and swung a fist toward my head.

55

It wasn't a hard punch. Her footing was off and so she didn't get enough leverage. I grabbed her other arm and pulled her off balance.

She hit the ground but managed to bring me down with her. I should have let go of her arm, but it all happened fast.

I recovered first and rolled on top of her. My weight would keep her down and make it impossible for her to lash out. Of course, I couldn't move either, or she'd be free. Unless I wanted to wait for the morning shift to arrive and help out, I needed to think fast.

Evelyn was trying to buck me off. Her hands were pressed to the ground at her sides, pushing her body up. It wasn't doing her any good. I was spread out on her back, and I was no lightweight.

I reached out and grabbed her right hand, scraping it along the concrete as I did. Then I maneuvered into position and tried for her left hand. She tried to roll me off, and it almost worked, but I rolled back and twisted her arm under my body. It wouldn't hold long. I needed her tied up. Not completely, but enough that I had control, and could walk her to my car.

I rolled to the left and reached again for her hand. She managed to keep it just out of my reach. I levered myself to standing and pulled her along by yanking the hand I still held.

Before she had a chance to jerk away, I brought her close and turned her back to me before twisting her arm again, forcing her to her knees.

I was in control unless she decided a broken arm and dislocated shoulder were worth her freedom. I didn't wait for her to choose. I wrenched her left arm from underneath, and she hung from my hands for a second before straightening.

The fight had happened in relative silence; a few grunts of pain didn't carry far enough to alarm anyone. I guess she was unwilling to have the cops called unless she controlled who came.

"We're going to my car," I said. "Don't give me any trouble and I won't hurt you any more than I already have."

"Fuck you."

Well, I didn't expect her to be happy about it, but now I figured holding her wrists wasn't going to be enough. I needed to tie her up, but there were no handy ropes nearby, and I didn't see any handcuffs on her belt.

Maybe I could pull her jacket down to hold her. I shoved her against the wall and leaned on her while I checked the pockets. My luck was holding. I found zip ties. She was planning to do this to me. Probably to make killing me easier.

I held her in place while I applied the restraints and then yanked her away from the wall. "Let's go."

"Where the fuck did you learn to fight like that?" She stumbled along as I dragged her by the zip ties.

"I've met too many people like you," I said. "I took lessons."

She dragged her feet and kept trying to pull away from me the entire block to my car.

"Okay, your choice. I can put you in the trunk, or in the passenger seat."

"Fine, I'll behave."

I didn't believe her, but I also didn't want to put her in the trunk. I opened the door, pushed her into the seat, and then used another zip tie to lock her to the door handle. When I thought she was secure, I pulled her seatbelt on and crossed the front of my car.

Since no one who could actually arrest her was answering my texts, I would have to drive her to the station. I sent a text to the group chat to say what I was doing, and then started the car.

"You won't get there," she said.

"How are you going to stop me?"

"Wonder why no one is answering?"

No; I'd been pissed but hadn't questioned it. "How do you know if no one is getting back to me?"

"You didn't think I came to meet you without a plan, did you?"

56

"**Y**ou don't seem worried," I said.

"I have a plan," Evelyn said.

Then a car sideswiped us.

A patrol car. Someone had been paying attention to my communications — just not the people on my team.

We were jammed against the hording around a development site. The impact had bashed a hole in the barrier right at the passenger door. I released my seatbelt and reached to do the same for Evelyn, but she'd beaten me to it. The force of the collision had snapped the zip tie I'd used to restrain her to the door. Her hands were still bound, but she was already pushing the door open.

It didn't give easily, so I had time to climb over the center console and add my weight to hers. I could hear someone coming from the other vehicle.

"Get the fuck out here, both of you," a man said. He didn't sound familiar, but I wasn't going to waste time and effort looking at him.

We got the door open enough to squish past it through

the hole in the hording. Whoever was after us would need to come through the car the same way we had.

I shoved Evelyn ahead of me, hoping a security guard would find us. Or at least that some lights would come on.

"In there," I said, nudging her toward a rotting basement door.

"I'll just wait here, if you don't mind," she said.

I pushed her harder so she would have to move. "They are after you as well. Didn't you hear him?"

"You think they're going to betray me now?" She kept moving despite her words.

"He wanted both of us out of the car," I said. "He's planning to kill us."

"No. He's rescuing me."

The last thing I needed was her calling out to the cop who was probably forcing his way through the gap behind us. "Why did he ram us rather than pulling us over? Is this how they killed Zoe? Are you really willing to take the chance?"

She pulled on the door and it creaked open. I ground my teeth at the noise. I knew it wouldn't be well-oiled, but it didn't need to signal our location so clearly.

I pulled out my phone and used the flashlight to check the area. "Over there. Behind the boiler. We'll be invisible unless he comes in and searches properly."

"You planning to turn us in, Moore?" Lucy Valette's voice. So, it wasn't just one rogue cop who'd come after us. Was Bill there too?

"See," I said.

"Then cut these restraints," Evelyn said, holding out her wrists. "I'm just a burden right now."

"No chance. We stay concealed until help arrives. Get in farther, I need to hide too."

I tried desperately not to think about spiders, or rats, or zombies, but my skin crawled anyway.

I turned the phone to face me so the light wouldn't give us away. I sent a text to Paul, but still no answer.

"Is my phone being blocked?" That was the only reason I could think of that would stop everyone from responding.

"Yeah."

So, no one was coming to our rescue. We'd need to escape and find a different phone.

"Do you have a phone?"

She nodded to her right hip pocket.

I pulled it out. Smashed during our fight. I dropped it into my pocket as evidence.

"We wait here until they move on and then we run. There'll be another way out of the site."

"Why don't you let them have me?"

"I'm not you. They'll kill you if I do that, and then they'll come for me. We need to get out and call for real help. Now shut up so I can listen for anyone approaching."

I leaned out around the boiler. There wasn't much to see, but the open door let in just enough light for me to make out shapes. Nothing human-sized moved. Leaving the door open wasn't the safest idea, but the noise and delay of closing it was too much of a risk.

I took the opportunity to glance around the basement. Boxes and a couple of plastic tubs filled the corners. A set of wooden steps rose to a door hanging on one hinge. If we were quiet, and lucky, maybe we could head upstairs and out a back door.

I nudged Evelyn and whispered the idea to her. She nodded, but I stopped her from moving. For now, she seemed willing to cooperate, but I knew that would change if she saw a chance to escape. Or could manufacture one by betraying me.

The basement door creaked and both of us froze. I couldn't peek; any movement would give us away.

"You see anything?" the man asked.

"Dirt, cobwebs, rat shit," Lucy answered. "Too dark to see much. You have a flashlight?"

"I'll get Bill to bring it from the cruiser. He's had time to clear the car from the hole in the hording."

So, we had a way out. If all three of them were here searching for us, we could make it to safety if we were given a tiny chance. Running would be better if I didn't need to think about pursuit. Of course, that meant we needed the chance, and we needed to get out without tipping them off.

"Let's meet him," Lucy said. "I'm not crazy about poking around in abandoned houses. He can check this place while we look around the other dumps."

Thank God for fussy murderers. I didn't hear anything for a few moments, so I leaned around again. No one silhouetted in the doorway. "Upstairs, fast and silent." I pulled Evelyn out of the corner, and we were in the kitchen within seconds. This time I took a moment to put the door back into place so we wouldn't signal our departure.

"Here is good," I said. "We'll go out the back door if they come."

"Okay, at least there's no spiderwebs here. Lots of rat shit though."

57

Rats didn't silently drop from the shadows to nest in your hair, so I was less worried about them than spiders. "Don't touch anything and stop talking."

The disadvantage of our new position was clear as soon as I settled into the space between the island and the cupboards. We couldn't hear anything, and there was no way to peep around a corner to get enough warning if we were about to be found. I nudged Evelyn closer to the back door, our only hope of escape.

I considered leading us out now while we were still alone. It was a risk, but I leaned around Evelyn to peek through the window in the top of the door. The moon was out, and no trees stood tall enough to hide anyone standing behind them.

The backyard was still clear, and the gate to the alley was broken off and rotting to the side of the opening. A fast run and we'd be clear. If we didn't trip over a hidden obstacle.

As I watched, the moon slid behind a cloud and something large moved in the dark. I tried to believe it was a stray dog, or a very large raccoon.

We wouldn't be quite so trapped outside as we were in the house, but we would have fewer places to hide.

"You need to cut the ties if you want me to run," Evelyn whispered. "I'll just slow you down."

I hadn't gone through all of this to set her free at the first problem — okay, not the first problem, but still.

We needed help whether we stayed here or made a run for it; there was little chance we'd escape three angry cops on the hunt. I pulled out my phone again. "Any chance that a call will go through?"

"They won't take the blocker off until they have us," Evelyn said. "They might not be as loyal as I thought, but my team is not stupid."

Evelyn's smashed phone was in my pocket, too. Maybe the damage was just to the screen. I brought up the fractured icon to make a call. The keyboard was unreadable. I wasn't sure that the nine and one were still in the same place. I hit the numbers anyway, but nothing happened.

"Moore, call out and we'll rescue you," Lucy shouted from not that far away.

I looked at Evelyn.

"Not a chance. They want me dead. If I'm gone, they think all the evidence can be laid on my corpse."

I got up from the floor and made Evelyn crouch beside me. We needed to run. I hoped the three cops would be reluctant to use their guns. The sound would carry to the houses nearby and surely someone would call 911, but we'd still be dead.

The two phones I held were the same brand. I slipped the protective case off mine and checked the side. I would need something to poke into the tiny hole that released the

SIM card. The likelihood of me or Evelyn having a paper clip in our pockets was less than nil.

"You have a pin or anything like that?" I asked.

"Why?"

"Just answer me."

"What do you think? It's not like I'm running around sewing quilts or collecting bugs."

I scanned the floor with my phone's flashlight beam carefully restricted between my palms. Someone had done a bit of demolition, and there were shards of plywood spread around. All too thick and fragile to use.

I held my breath and listened carefully. No sound of anyone approaching, so I rose a little and started opening drawers. Whoever lived here hadn't packed everything before they moved. A bent fork hugged the corner of the first drawer. Too thick. A handful of twist ties hid in the back of the drawer. I pulled them out and ducked back into my crouch.

"I'm cramping," Evelyn said.

"Fine, sit down for a second." I peeled the paper back from the wire inside the twist tie then poked my finger to make sure it would stay stiff enough to work.

Evelyn shifted beside me.

"Don't try to run. You'll be caught before you get down the steps."

She stopped moving.

I used the twist tie to open the SIM tray on Evelyn's phone. The card was undamaged. I placed it carefully on my knee and did the same with mine. Then I put her SIM card in my phone, saying a prayer that we wouldn't be locked out for an hour because of the change.

I looked over at Evelyn before I did anything. "What are the chances they've blocked your phone?"

Her grin told me nothing. It could be that she was happy I found a way to call for help, or that she was setting me up. "Maybe, but I had the access code to the system."

I hit David's number and waited. If he decided to ignore a call from Evelyn, I'd send a text to tell him to pick up.

He answered, and before he could speak, I said, "It's me."

"Charity, where the fuck are you?"

I'd never been so happy to be yelled at.

58

"I'm hiding in an abandoned house in a development near Hastings and Clark. My car is rammed into the hording. Or maybe it's moved now?"

"Alone?" I heard him say something to another person but couldn't make out the words.

"No. I've got Evelyn Moore in restraints, ready to take in. But the other three cops Paul and I identified are kind of hunting us down."

"Stay where you are and don't come out until I yell for you."

If he was at the station, we only needed to stay alive and free for about ten minutes at this time of night. Easy enough if we weren't found by any of the three cops searching for us. All it would take is one mistake or one stroke of bad luck to be captured. If they didn't kill us right away, we'd be hostages — at least I would be; I wasn't sure how they'd treat Evelyn.

"Stay very quiet and still," I said.

Our luck wasn't exactly holding, because the next thing I

heard came from outside and was accompanied by a bright light shining against the wall.

"We stick together," Lucy said.

Interesting that women ran this crew.

Evelyn leaned into me and whispered, "We need to run."

"No. Just be silent."

We listened to the three of them argue for what felt like hours, but could only have been five minutes or so because there were no sirens. The flashlight showed us the route they took around the house, shining in through the dusty windows at an angle that meant they were still on the ground.

I'd been holding my breath and needed to inhale again without gasping or coughing or making any kind of noise to attract their interest.

"I'm going up," Bill said. "We can't see anything from here."

The houses were close enough together that I couldn't be sure which one Bill was about to enter. I sank down as low as possible to avoid being seen, then jerked on Evelyn's sleeve to pull her away from the edge.

If Bill was at this house, and he just looked through the window, maybe he wouldn't be able to see us. I desperately wanted to check the time, but no amount of cover would hide the light of my phone screen.

"Hey!"

Lucy again. Then a scuffle, and then heavy footsteps racing up the stairs to our back door. I scanned for something to use as a weapon, but no cupboard door or shelf lay at hand.

The back door screeched open, and someone stood in the sudden brightness.

"Charity?"

It was David. We were safe.

I answered him and tried to stand gracefully without using the rat-dropping covered floor to push up, but no dice. I was going to be in the shower until the hot water ran out.

"They're here," David called back over his shoulder.

He took my hand and pulled me in close for a hug, then reached for Evelyn, who was trying to escape to the basement. Ungrateful bitch.

Outside, I was greeted by the sight of ten or more cops in uniforms and plain clothes. Paul waved at me and ended a conversation he was having with an older cop. I saw Bill being assisted into the back of a cruiser, but the other two must already be gone.

"There's an ambulance on its way. Just to check you out," he said. "Unless there's a need to put you in hospital." He sounded like that was exactly what he wanted. Me in a ward, all tucked away and not interfering.

David handed Evelyn off to one of the cops and joined us.

"This is done now, right?" he asked Paul. "You've finished putting Charity in danger for your own purposes?"

"What?" I said. "He was working with me, David. He wasn't responsible for this situation. I tried to call and text everyone, but they jammed my phone."

"Yeah, he didn't mention he was transferred to Professional Standards? That this was all a sting to get the identities of a corrupt gang of cops?"

I looked at Paul and saw the truth on his face. "You asshole. I trusted you, and this was all lies. Did you get Rance to hire me? Is it all bullshit?"

Paul stepped back out of fist-range, as if I was stupid enough to punch him with so many witnesses.

"No. No one knew I was working this as a case, Charity.

You got hired by Rance and we saw the opportunity. I had no idea who the leader was. The investigation was legitimate."

I turned away from him. I knew trusting cops was a bad idea; why did I get sucked in every time?

David took my arm and steered me toward the ambulance, where I used as much of the sanitizing gel as they would let me.

59

They let me go home in David's custody — they said his 'care', but I knew better. I sent my report to Rance and then slept through to ten in the morning, and actually started to feel more like myself.

Now we were at the VPD station. David insisted on being with me for the interview, perhaps because he thought the Professional Standards people needed protection.

At least I wasn't in an interrogation cell. The conference room wasn't luxurious, but it was larger than the last one. The table was set up to hold ten people, with water and coffee in the middle. Paul was across from me and David. The boss, an old guy named Cyril something, was at the head of the table.

I waited for them to start the meeting. I think they were waiting for me to do the same. We'd see who could waste the most time.

I won when Paul glanced at his boss and then looked back to me. "Let me explain what we were doing."

I nodded and waited. He must know how angry I was, but there was no sense of it in his voice or posture.

"Professional Standards has known for some time that we had a corruption problem. We had rumors, but nothing concrete. That's how it usually starts with this department. When Rance started complaining about Joan Tiller being framed, we saw an opportunity."

"Why didn't you tell me this to start with?" If he thought my anger was about anything but him betraying my trust, he was in for a shock. David patted my hand — in reassurance, I hoped, but it could have been a reminder to stay calm.

"I'm sorry I had to keep it to myself. My transfer to Professional Standards wasn't announced yet. The bosses thought it was an advantage."

"You do get why no one likes you, right? The department, I mean. Too many lies."

Cyril pushed a sheet of paper toward me. "We have informed MacDonald that his client has been released. Your contract with him is fulfilled."

I looked down at the paper. It was a consultancy contract. "I'm not working with you." I pushed it back.

"You do good work. Unconventional, and a little too far into the gray areas sometimes, but you get results."

"I won't as soon as people find out I work for you." I was not going to be dragged into their mess.

David took my hand and gave it a squeeze. "Charity works best on her own," he said.

"I understand. You can't blame me for trying," Cyril said. He stood. "Grewal, I expect you in my office in ten." He grabbed the contract and left us alone.

"Charity, I'm so sorry you got into that much danger. If I had any idea what was going down, I would never have left you."

"You lied to me, Paul. You were reporting back everything we did. Did you have to ask permission to bring me the files? To give me access to the information we needed? We could have solved this days ago if you'd been up front." I stopped talking because I could feel my temper tipping over the edge.

"It's no excuse, but I tried to tell them all of that. Professional Standards isn't a really trusting department."

"And Zoe?"

He looked away and rubbed his face.

"Charity," David said, "he doesn't need you to tell him he screwed up to make him feel worse."

He was right. I was sure Paul was beating himself up over Zoe's death. "I feel like shit about it too. But maybe she was going to be murdered before we got involved. I can't help but think she wouldn't be dead if we'd been faster."

Paul nodded at David. "You are probably right, but if we'd been quicker to solve the case, I don't think it would be as solid. I feel like we let her down, and we were partly responsible, but she made her choices. She's not the only face I see when I try to sleep at night."

Now I felt sorry for him. He was a good cop. He had a job to do, and maybe I didn't like being used, but it wasn't his choice. And he had introduced me to that great restaurant — or at least a new side of one I thought I knew.

"I can't work with the cops again," I said. "I'm not cut out for all the rules and all the casual violations of the rules. All the deception."

"Fair enough," Paul said.

Why did I feel like he meant that they'd come up with a compelling reason when they wanted me back?

"Good luck in your new job," I said.

60

We went from the VPD to the North Shore to get some baby time and lunch. Lu and Matthieu had a delicious looking spread of finger food and full-sized wine on the patio table. My favorite way to eat, because I could have tiny sandwiches and chocolate strawberries together, with no rules about waiting for dessert. And I had a designated driver.

"You can't hold a grudge forever," David said.

"You feel like putting money on that?" I asked. "How come you didn't know about Paul's move to Professional Standards? Or did you know, and keep it secret?"

"I'm pretty sure Leigh and I were purposely kept in the dark. It's not unusual for a first case in Professional Standards to conclude before the announcement. I am surprised that Moore didn't know." He put a tiny salmon sandwich on my plate. "I would never lie to you, Charity, not about something this important."

I hadn't been serious, but I felt a flood of relief when he confirmed he was on my team. "What happens to Evelyn's boss, Ted Johnson? We thought he might be the leader for a while."

David reached for a pickle before answering. "He'll be investigated to be sure, but he put in his retirement papers today. Unless there's strong evidence against him, that will be the end of it."

"I guess that's the last thread to tie up. Let me snuggle Theo for a few minutes to reset my brain from pissed off to happy."

I lifted the baby from his seat and snuggled him, taking a sniff of his head. It didn't take more than ten seconds to get me out of the past and thinking about the future. I was happy to get tiny sips of baby love and let Lu have all the rest, including sleepless nights, diaper changes, and colic. She looked at me with a smile and tipped her head toward David. I guess he passed her test.

"I got a call from Rance," Matthieu said. "He has an offer for us."

I took a sip of my wine and a bite of chocolate. "More work?"

"He's offering us a contract to do the investigative work for his firm."

"What happened to the usual people he uses?" I wasn't going to turn down steady work, but if there was a problem, I needed to know.

"Still there," Matthieu said. "The firm needs more investigators because they are expanding their services. We would specialize in the criminal cases. The other team will work more with the financial fraud lawyers."

Steady work meant I wouldn't be looking for clients so often. "What about the regular clients we have now? I can't take on more work by myself."

"I will come back. Or rather, I will work from home so I can be with my son. We will sort out how it will work."

I looked at Lu to see how she felt. Matthieu deciding to come back to work so soon after saying he wanted to spend more time with family felt a little like trouble.

"I'm getting a nanny," she said. "Theo isn't enough trouble for either of us. I'm going back to my nonprofit work. We'll both do it from home for the most part, so we will be with him even when the nanny is here."

I had no idea if that was an easy decision or not. It made sense to me. A great balance between parenting and adulting. "Okay. I'll get the details from Rance tomorrow. I'm looking forward to some nice, boring cases. Ones where no one is trying to kill me."

WANT MORE?

If you liked this book, you might like other books in the series, check out all my mystery/thrillers, by using the QR code to head over to my website.

If you enjoyed reading CONVICTION please consider helping other readers to find the story by leaving a review.

FREE EBOOK

Claim your copy of Buying Into Death when you use the QR code to sign up for my newsletter and follow Charity as she solves her fastest case yet!

Or... Head over to www.pawilson.ca/mysteries and sign up.

ALSO BY P A WILSON

For more books by P A Wilson

Use the QR code below or go to pawilson.ca

ABOUT THE AUTHOR

Perry Wilson is a Canadian author based in Vancouver, BC who has big ideas and an itch to tell stories. Having spent some time on university, a career, and life in general, she returned to writing in 2008 and hasn't looked back since (well, maybe a little, but only while parallel parking).

She is a member of the Vancouver Writers Social Group, The Royal City Literary Arts Society, and The Surrey Writing Workshop. Perry has self-published several novels. She writes the Madeline Journeys, a fantasy series about a high-powered lawyer who finds herself trapped in a magical world, the Quinn Larson Quests, which follows the adventures of a wizard named Quinn who must contend with volatile fae in the heart of Vancouver, and the Charity Deacon Investigations, a mystery thriller series about a private eye who tends to fall into serious trouble with her cases, and The Riverton Romances, a series based in a small town in Oregon, one of her favorite states. Her stand-alone novels are Breaking the Bonds, Closing the Circle, and The Dragon at The Edge of The Map.

For more information
www.pawilson.ca
pawilson@pawilson.ca

ACKNOWLEDGMENTS

People think that the process of writing is solitary. That's not the case for me. I have help from so many people it would be hard to acknowledge everyone, but I'll give it a try.

The support and inspiration I get from my writer's groups is incalculable. The Vancouver Writers Social Group opens my mind to other ways of telling a story. The Royal City Literary Arts Society gives me the opportunity to meet and share with other writers who have more knowledge than I do. The Other 11 Months group is where I learn about getting the words on the page. And my critique group who helps me find the best parts of the story I want to tell. Thanks to all of the members of these great groups.

Last of all, but definitely a huge part of the process, my beta readers. These are the people who love stories and are willing, and more than able, to tell me if my finished story is ready for you, my readers.